THE KILLER

Jack Elgos

YELLOWBAY BOOKS

Published by YellowBay Books Ltd 2012
www.yellowbay.co.uk

Copyright © Jack Elgos 2012

YellowBay Books Ltd
ISBN 9 7 8 1 9 0 8 5 3 0 3 9 4

Cover design by Emily Heaton

YellowBay Books is dedicated to edgy, daring and radical new
writing.
Let us know what you think at **info@yellowbay.co.uk**,
Or visit Amazon and give the book a review

*"When starting down the road of revenge,
you must first dig two graves."*

This man disagrees with Confucius. He knows that two graves won't be nearly enough.

1

England, 1985

Just before dawn in the half-light of day, he rubbed a small circle of condensation from the ice-cold windowpane. 'Only the needy and the greedy are out today Liam me lad,' he whispered quietly as he shivered. Gazing out over the bleak landscape he took a deep, satisfying drag from one of his favourite fags, Capstan full strength. 'Ah Jesus, what a miserable cold, grey day,' he sighed as he continued to stare out at the light rain drizzling slowly down onto the mist-covered fields surrounding the old Derbyshire manor house. Everything was quiet.

Draining the remains of a strong black coffee, he struggled to counter the pounding effects of last night's bottle of Jameson as he took his place at the old desk and started his daily ritual of stripping and thoroughly cleaning today's weapon of choice. Closing his eyes he picked up the piece and engaged the safety. He removed the mag and cocking handle, continued with the butt and grip, then finally the retracting bolt head assembly and recoil spring.

Only when the HK MP5 was broken down into all its parts did he open his eyes to inspect every single component. He then cleaned and oiled each piece individually. 'Clinical cleanliness always, Liam,' he repeated to himself as he sat in the eerie grey glow coming from the bank of security monitors. He was about to close his eyes once more to rebuild the MP5 when something caught his attention and a glance at the monitors confirmed the movement. A car was approaching. Springing from his seat he watched a silver Mercedes saloon car making its way down the long drive. Finally it arrived and parked next to his Jaguar, directly opposite his front door.

The bell rang twice. Checking the monitors for any further movement Liam, a 9mm pistol in his right hand, cautiously eased open the door with his left. The visitor stood and nodded. Neither man uttered a word of greeting as Turner entered and strolled across to the drawing room. Liam secured the front door again before following and eventually taking his seat behind the antique mahogany desk. In total silence Turner took the seat opposite then, opening his briefcase, he slid a large envelope in the direction of Liam who grabbed it, tore it open and pulled out the sheaf of printed documents.

Page after page he studied the contents of times, dates and locations. Finally he arrived at the collection of images; cars, houses and offices along with their associated blueprints. Then he saw a photograph with the face of his new target. 'Jesus, Mary and Joseph,' Liam thought. 'I'd happily hit this bastard for free.'

Showing no emotion at the picture of a man he recognised only too well, he looked directly at Turner asking, 'Same money?'

'Yes, of course old chap, the same money as always,' nodded Turner. 'However, this one will carry a bit of a bonus. It cannot appear to be an accident, I'm afraid. It has to be a very public affair.'

'Why in public?' Liam asked, his fingers tracing the line of the old crescent shaped scar on his cheek.

'Orders,' Turner replied. 'You have all the information you need. The transfer of funds will be made when the work has been completed and the termination is confirmed.' Turner stood and waited for the briefest of moments, should there be any further questions. There were none. He turned and left without uttering another word.

Locking the door once more Liam watched as the Mercedes exited the driveway and then he returned to the drawing room where he studied the security monitors. Nothing. Once again all was quiet, just as it should be.

2

The Beginning:
Northern Ireland, 1978

Butch knew all there was to know about survival; he was an expert. Having grown up in Belfast, one of the most dangerous cities in the world, violence had been his constant companion. A little short of stature and a bit underweight he had been the target of bullies, but his early years brawling on the streets had taught him how to survive in this brutal, segregated city. In his late teens he'd perfected his own unique form of street fighting, turning it into a virtual art form. By the time he'd reached his mid twenties he'd earned the reputation as a violent man, one best avoided. Though he didn't know it at the time Butch was soon to become one of the most feared of Belfast's many hard-men.

Despite their constant attempts to recruit him, Butch had always refused the Provos with a firm, 'Look, fuck off boys; you know I'm not political. Go fight your own war.' As if to make sure they fully understood his position he'd fight just as hard with the Catholic boys as he would with the Protestants.

'Darren, my son, as long as I draw breath, promise me you'll not get involved in the troubles.' His mother's constant words echoed through his mind at every attempted recruitment. Strange to think back then that everyone still called him Darren. He wished they still would. He hated the name Butch.

Then, one dark, cold and rainy night, a Proddy outfit abducted and murdered his mother. Mrs. McCann was making her way home from visiting friends when she had been viciously attacked. She was brutally beaten and her throat was cut. Everyone in the province assumed the attack was a punishment. Her crime? She was Catholic.

This, signature killing, was clearly the work of a specific Protestant Paramilitary squad: the infamous Shankill Butchers. The squad took their orders directly from The Ulster Volunteer Force, a loyalist paramilitary group. Though never actually claiming responsibility for the killing, the method used put the blame firmly at the doorstep of the U.V.F.

From the moment her body had been found, Darren McCann was transformed from a lone street fighter. Heartbroken at the loss of his beloved mother, his feelings of hatred towards her killers made him the perfect weapon for the Republicans. He was recruited into the Provisional I.R.A. the day following his mother's funeral.

***

The Training Camp - For One

Several weeks later, Darren peeped out of the front door and smiled. He wasn't altogether shocked, but he was pleasantly surprised. After spending several minutes checking both directions of Nansen Street he found there was not one soldier to be seen. In his vivid nightmare last night he'd opened this door to face hundreds of police and soldiers all waiting to take him, the latest recruit for the I.R.A., and lock him away forever - in the dreaded H-Blocks. He breathed a huge sigh of relief as he realised it really had been nothing but a bad dream.

He spent the day fidgeting and pacing, waiting for the allotted hour yet dreading it at the same time. His nightmare kept coming back to haunt him and his disturbed sleep had left him weary and anxious. Eventually, some time in the afternoon, he felt himself nodding off and sat back in a chair for the quick nap he knew he needed.

The sun was low in the sky when he opened his eyes again and a quick glance at his watch confirmed that he was late. 'Fuck, wake up you stupid idiot, you're not gonna make it.' He set off walking quickly down Nansen Street, but as he reached the junction he knew he could never make up the time at this pace. Once onto the Falls Road he started to run, which in Belfast was not a healthy thing to do. Most runners seen on these streets were running away from something - like a shooting, or a bombing. They were definitely not taking their evening jog.

Running was something Darren rarely did. He never liked to run to, or away from, anything or anyone - but this was different. This evening he was running to meet some scary people. Not the type of scary people he'd fight with in Belfast's pubs and bars, these were *really* scary people and he didn't want to be late for the meeting. When he reached the pick up point he checked his watch and he'd made it with five minutes to spare. 'Thank God for that,' he whispered.

As he sat on the pavement and waited he noticed four other young men. Briefly they made eye contact, but quickly broke it, each one finding a new spot on which to lock his gaze. These young men had all volunteered and they had individually been told the number one rule, 'Do not talk to anyone, ever.' Though still sweating, Darren began to relax a little. He lit a cigarette, inhaling the smoke deep into his lungs.

A Transit van pulled up. A short, fat man climbed out of the passenger side, moved to the rear of the van and opened its back doors. Eyeing the five waiting men he stared at them in turn. When he finally spoke, the briefness of his instruction only served to underline his command. 'Get in!'

They all climbed in and took a seat. 'No talking,' the man hissed. 'I hear anyone utter a fucking word - and they don't make it.' Opening his jacket a little for effect, they each caught a glimpse of the pistol he showed them. Inwardly Darren shivered.

The journey was interrupted four times and the other men were dropped off at stages along the route until Darren was the only one left in the vehicle. A short drive on rough roads followed and, as the van came to a final, abrupt stop, he could hear shouting. A moment later and the rear doors swung quickly open. Darren had arrived in darkness. Though he had been told he was to be sent to Derry, the pitch black of the night left him with absolutely no idea where he was. He could've been anywhere really. But he knew he was still in Ireland: he could feel it.

'Out now!' Someone unseen barked the order to him. Climbing out of the van Darren stood trying to survey his new home. 'Not much to look at,' he thought, as his eyes slowly adjusted to the gloom. Then he was blinded again, as a bright light shone directly into his face.

'Welcome to Derry, McCann,' the man said in a deep County Armagh accent. 'You're in the Provos now,' he announced as he inspected the new recruit. Darren sprang to attention until the voice eventually ordered, 'OK, follow me son.'

Darren did as he was told, following the man into a dark old barn. As they entered the man reached out and flicked a switch, illuminating the area, and Darren's eyes widened in surprise. Though from the outside it looked like any old farm building, the interior looked anything but. It was spotlessly clean and on the concrete floor stood four long tables, each covered in a green tarpaulin.

The man pointed to the corner of the room at three doors. 'Your room is the last one on the left,' he informed him. Then he turned to leave with a friendly 'goodnight', and Darren was alone.

When he entered his room, Darren was pleasantly surprised to see a small stove, a kettle, a fridge - and a bed. He opened the fridge door and stood smiling, whispering, 'Thank God for that.' He'd not eaten for many hours and the sight of bread, bacon, eggs and milk made his mouth water.

As he swallowed the last of his sandwich and drained the remainder of his tea, he burped loudly and crawled slowly into bed. This had been one very long day.

The following morning his dreams were interrupted by a loud crash and bright, blinding light as the door flew open and banged into the wall. 'Up and dressed McCann,' he heard Mr. County Armagh shout. Darren jumped from his bed and immediately drew in his breath as the cold assaulted him. It was freezing. Following a rushed wash in icy water he quickly dressed and hurried to the main area of the barn. There he found the man waiting for him, clothed in camouflage gear. Darren jumped to attention and offered his best salute.

'Relax lad,' the man told him, a friendly smile on his face. 'I don't know what you were expecting, but marching up and down all day like toy soldiers is not what's done here.'

Darren lowered his arm. 'So, where is here and what, exactly, is done then?' he asked.

'We're close to the Derry area, or thereabouts son. That's all you need to know about where we are. And here we, or rather I, will train you to fight and to kill. Here you'll learn how to kill in the most effective manner possible.' The man smiled. 'My name is Collins,' he added.

'Am I the only one here Mr. Collins?' Darren asked as he scanned the room, looking for other recruits.

'Yes son, there is only ever one person here at a time. The training is done on a one on one basis. And, by the way, the name's Collins. Not Mr., not Captain - just make it Collins.'

'OK then - Collins, what's first?'

'First son, I need to know a little about you. Why are you here, and what are you good at?' he asked his latest recruit as he poured two cups of tea. 'Milk and sugar?' he offered with another smile.

Darren wasn't sure what he had expected, but sitting and chatting over a nice warm brew definitely wasn't it, not that he was complaining. The chat grew dark, though, as he filled Collins in on his mam's murder. Then, clenching his fists, he told him what he did well. Basically, this boiled down to fighting, and winning.

'So, you're here for revenge then eh lad?'

'Aye, that I am. I joined to kill those Shankill bastards, every one of them,' he spat.

'I've read your report,' Collins confirmed. 'It says you're a good street fighter lad. A hard case, good with your fists - but fists against bullets is not the way I'd want to go.'

'It's not just my fists,' Darren assured him, 'I'll use anything I can find to put a man down; bottles, bricks, knives – anything.'

'Guns?' asked Collins.

'No, sir, I've never even held a gun. Promised my mammy that I wouldn't get involved in any shootings you see.'

'But now she's gone, and you want to learn, eh lad?'

'Aye, that I do. I want to learn everything you can teach me,' he replied seriously.

'Right, have you finished your tea? Then let's start laddie,' Collins commanded as he stood, pulling the tarpaulin from one of the smaller tables. 'This,' he picked up a gun, 'is a Browning .45 automatic pistol.'

The remainder of the day was spent with lessons repeated over and over, stripping, rebuilding and firing an assortment of small handguns. Darren studied hard, copying the man with every breakdown and rebuild of each weapon. At every procedure Collins would stare him directly in the face, firmly reminding him of his favourite saying: 'Clinical cleanliness always, son.'

That mantra, Collins informed him, had been drilled into the head of many a raw recruit who had passed through his hands. 'To the best of my knowledge, lad, it has served them all well.' Then he continued, driving the fact into Darren's head, constantly reminding him that, 'It's the only way to go - any dirt in any firearm, especially an automatic, can result in a jam - and a gun jamming on you will probably cost you your life.'

The following morning began in exactly the same manner as the previous one. First the tea - then the chat. As he sipped his tea Collins glanced over the cup. 'So, you want to have a go at the Shankill boys do you lad?' Darren nodded enthusiastically.

'But, you are aware that The Butchers take their orders from the U.V.F. aren't you?'

Again, Darren nodded. 'Of course I am.'

'Then you need to broaden your outlook a little son,' advised Collins. 'It's not just The Butchers who are responsible,' he explained patiently.

'It is for me,' replied Darren.

Collins, reclining a little in his seat, took a deep breath, then in a softer tone explained, 'Look son, we're not just fighting The Butchers or U.V.F. you know. We're fighting the fucking lot of them. The U.D.A., The U.V.F. and the Brits - everyone. It wasn't just one group that killed your mam, it was all of them - they're all the same.'

Glancing up at Collins, Darren frowned at him in an effort to clarify his reasons. 'I know that, but it was The Butchers who murdered mammy, and that's who I want.'

'But where do you think The Butchers get their finance from son? Their arms, their ammo, their finance, their intelligence - they're supplied by the fucking U.V.F. And they, in turn, are supplied by the fucking British Government. It's each and every single loyalist paramilitary outfit we're fighting. And the biggest threat of all comes directly from the Brits. Without support from the British there would be no threat - without the British support your mam would probably still be alive.'

He'd never thought about it in this way. The man's words started making sense to him and, for the briefest of seconds, Darren's eyes began watering a little. Quickly he blinked the tears away before looking back at his instructor. 'If you really want someone to blame for your mother's murder - look no further than the British: they're your real enemy,' Collins told him. 'Because ultimately the blame for her death lies with them - can you see that now son?' At the slight nod from his pupil he changed the subject, noting the sadness in the lad's face. 'Anyhow, enough of all that, let's get on and make a start on today's training.' Striding over to another table he dragged the tarp off and announced, 'Today, bolt action rifles, shotguns and assault rifles.'

This specialist arms training continued for six more, very long, weeks. As he neared the end of the course Darren was happy to find that he could efficiently field strip, clean and reassemble virtually any firearm presented to him.

'Well done lad,' Collins announced as Darren completed his last rebuild, 'but, you do realise that it won't always be daylight when you need to strip a weapon don't you?'

Confused, Darren stared at his trainer. 'Well, aye, but how do you mean?' he asked.

Collins pulled a long, black piece of cloth from his pocket as he told him, 'Now, do it again - but this time do it blindfolded.'

'Bollocks,' thought Darren, but Collins had already covered his eyes in one swift movement.

Now, unable to see anything at all, Darren sat and listened to his instructor. 'I need you to tell me the manufacturer, type and firing rate of this weapon. I need to know the ammunition it uses, which mag it fits, how many rounds per mag. You are then to strip, clean and rebuild it. Then, make it ready for firing.'

He couldn't believe this. Sure what the man said made sense, but fuck, this seemed impossible. Still, he attempted to field strip the rifle - using only his sense of touch. The total blackness hampered him, to say the least, and he made a total mess of it.

'Practice, practice and more practice lad. You need to recognise any weapon at hand, by feel alone - you'll get it.'

Two weeks later and Darren sat, blindfolded but with a beaming grin on his face, as he completed the last rebuild of the day. Now he could tell Collins everything about any weapon. From its size, weight and smell he knew each one individually as they were handed to him, one after the other. He knew them all and he could distinguish the individual ammo each weapon used. Darkness had become his friend.

Collins was delighted with the lad's performance. Whoever had recommended this particular young feller had chosen wisely, for the lad was a natural. He proved to be a fair shot too, but in the world of automatic weapons the ability to clear a jammed gun quickly and efficiently was far more use than precise, sniper type accuracy. This lad would do well and he would follow his career with interest and hope. Of course, they all disappeared into the shadowy underworld eventually, but he would keep tabs for as long as he could. That was the interesting part. The hope, though, went far deeper. That hope was for continued loyalty, and Collins quickly banished the memory of the one who had "turned".

***

Morals?

His final week was fast approaching and, following their daily ritual of tea and a chat, Collins announced, 'Today's lesson – explosives,' as he pulled the tarp from the last table revealing all manor of explosives, cables, timers and other devices that were completely unknown to Darren.

He looked down at the table, then back up at his trainer. A second or two later he told him, 'I'll not be needing this lesson,' adding firmly, 'I won't use explosives.'

Collins returned the look with a stare. 'What?' he asked incredulously. 'You won't use explosives? Who the fuck do you think you are? What the fuck are you talking about man?'

Darren gave him a direct, serious glare and told him, 'Look, I won't blow any poor fucker to bits. Sure I'll fight them, stab them, shoot them and kill them - I have no problem with any of that. But I won't stand miles away and kill a man like a coward.'

'You will do as ordered,' snapped Collins. 'You will learn this and you will use them if, and when, you are ordered to - is that clear McCann?'

'No sir,' Darren said firmly. 'I certainly will not.'

Collins stammered. He couldn't believe what he was hearing. 'You will do as you are told. You are a soldier of the I.R-fucking-A. Do you fucking understand me McCann?'

Darren held his stare, calmly replying, 'No, I won't - I'll not use bombs on people. I'm a fighter, not a fucking coward.'

'Back to the autos,' screamed Collins as he pointed at the rifle table. 'Strip, clean and rebuild every one. When you're finished, start on the hand guns, and when you're finished with that - do it all over again.' Angrily, he marched out of the room, scowling all the way.

Darren sat in front of the "auto" table and placed the blindfold over his eyes. Then he set about stripping the first rifle he picked up. 'AK 47,' he said to himself, before adding quietly, 'paratrooper version,' as his fingers fondled the rifle's hinge and skeleton stock.

Inside the farmhouse Collins sat stiffly. He began blowing gently onto his tea in an effort to cool his anger as much as the steaming brew. The man sitting opposite him was quiet, patiently waiting. Collins simply stared.

'Well - if he won't, he won't, simple as that,' the man stated.

'Yes, but he's blatantly refusing a direct, fucking order,' snapped Collins.

'Look Davy, the lad obviously has a problem with the use of explosives. He's already told you he's ready to kill, but only on his terms. And, like all of them, he is, after all, a volunteer. Why don't you cut him a little slack and let him go fight - in his own way. We really do need them all you know.'

'Is that your answer, to simply let him do as he likes, and miss explosives altogether?' asked Collins.

'Yes, it is. He's finished firearms training in top form, you said so yourself. Cut him loose and send him back - there are plenty more young lads waiting. I'm sure the next one won't be so picky.'

'Is that a direct order?' Collins asked.

'Yes Davy, consider it an order.'

'Fine, he'll leave tomorrow then. You know I was starting to really like this guy, but after today's little outburst I can't wait to see the back of him,' Collins told his superior.

'That's fine Davy. I'll arrange for your next boy to be collected by the same transport he leaves on.'

The following morning Darren left the camp near Derry. 'Goodbye and thank you for everything Collins,' he whispered as the van drove him away. Finally he was heading back home to Belfast and he hoped he'd be ordered directly into active service. He was ready, he was able and he was way more than willing to kill whomever he was ordered. Collins had been right – they were all his enemies. It would be nice if he could get a go at them Shankill bastards, though. He smiled in anticipation.

3

Active Service

Darren didn't have long to wait for his first orders and, over the next few months, he honed his craft, carrying out his directives efficiently. He was happiest when he worked alone. He liked to carry out his own reconnaissance, seeing the job through to the end, and he quickly had several sniper kills to his credit. The solitude part appealed to him. Teamwork – not so much, but sometimes those were the orders.

He was still new to the cause when he saw his first interrogation. The beating he witnessed sickened him in the beginning, offending his belief in a fair fight. A guy strapped to a chair didn't stand a chance, yet it was effective as the man quickly admitted his betrayal and was rewarded with a swift death. At his second interrogation, Darren was more than just an onlooker. Subject number two was far more resilient and all hands were needed before he finally gave up what he knew. With interrogation number three he was fully employed and this guy gave up nothing. Darren wasn't sure he knew anything to give up, but one thing became clear. If a man refuses to talk to you, then he talks to no one. The death of subject number three was inevitable and Darren was the one to finish the job, which he did without flinching. He knew he had changed. He'd been a tough guy to begin with, but even his dear, departed mother wouldn't recognise him now. He wasn't sure he recognised himself.

It was roughly six months after he had left the training camp when Duggy Mallone came to find him. 'Have you seen the news, McCann?' he asked, as he scanned the small room Darren called home. 'Where's your TV?'

'Don't have any use for one.'

'How do you know what's going on, then?'

'People like you come and tell me.'

'Ah.'

'Like you've something to tell me now?' Darren suggested.

'Oh, aye, sure. Everyone's talking about it. You know Calum O'Connell?' Darren nodded at the name of the well-known and highly placed I.R.A. sympathiser. 'Well, they've done for him, man,' Duggy continued. 'Those Shankill bastards, and they really went to town. Gutted, he was, but that's not the worst of it. They took out his wife and kid too. Slashed their throats.'

Darren winced. That was against the code. Each man lived by what he believed and was willing to die for it. Often they were slaughtered in front of their families to make a point, but to kill the family was beyond the pale and images of his own mother, her neck slit open, rushed to his brain. 'Bastards,' he spat.

'Aye,' Duggy agreed.

The police search for the culprit went on for weeks, but they would never find him. Just two days after the atrocity, news reached Darren that the boys had him and he raced to the scene. At a few minutes before midnight he entered an old, boarded up house and descended the stairs to the damp, cold cellar where the unmistakable odours of blood, sweat and human shit assaulted his nostrils. In the dimly lit interior a tall, bearded, tattooed man stood over a figure strapped to a chair, the face bloodied and beaten.

'The man with the beard is wanting to extract much information before the kill,' a strangely accented voice whispered from the shadows.

'What has he said so far?' Darren wanted to know.

'Exactly nothing,' said the voice.

'Not a word?'

'Oh, many words, yes, but this we already know.'

'Like what?' Darren pressed.

'He is Shankill Butcher, yes. He killed the man, yes. He killed the woman and the boy, yes. He has killed many others, yes. He will tell the hairy man who they were, no.'

Darren watched as a fist connected with the disfigured face, blood flying from the broken nose. 'How many others?' came the question that had clearly been asked several times before. There was no reply, just two bloodshot eyes staring defiantly from rearranged features. This man could take a beating, Darren had to acknowledge, as he stared at the first Shankill Butcher he had knowingly encountered in the flesh. He felt his pulse rate quicken as he thought of his mam and the fate she had endured at the hands of men such as him.

Darren moved slowly into the room. 'How many women?' he asked from behind the tattooed arm raised in preparation for another blow. A bloodied face and a bearded face stared at him in equal surprise.

'Who the fuck are you?' slurred the bloody one through broken teeth.

'How many women?' Darren repeated, roughly pushing aside the large, imposing interrogator.

It seemed the tattooed fist was now aimed in his direction, but another hand restrained it, offering in that strange accent, 'Let the boy try.'

Darren bent low, his face coming close to the one in the chair. 'How about Mary McCann?'

'Who?'

'Mary Jeanette McCann.'

'Never heard of her,' came the reply. 'Who was she? Some Catholic whore?'

It was as though someone had flicked a switch in Darren's brain. He stood away from the chair, arched his back and howled at the ceiling before reaching into his back pocket to remove the knife he always kept there for protection. In two swift movements he had slashed the Shankill Butcher across each cheek. 'Mary Jeanette McCann,' he screamed. 'My mother.'

'No, no. I don't know. I don't know her,' came the reply. It was difficult to make out the words now through the gaping mouth, but the fear was finally evident in the voice that rose to a shrill scream as Darren reached out to hold the man's ear and began to hack at it with the knife that was a little too blunt for the job.

The Shankill Butcher gave up no further information. He couldn't, as Darren slowly cut his face to pieces. Those in the room; a tall, bearded, tattooed man and three battle-hardened Provo activists, would later report having left the cellar before the job was finished, two of them even admitting to vomiting outside. Only one man, a short, stocky Spaniard, stayed to witness the whole thing. Just before midnight, Darren McCann had entered an old, boarded up building, but as the sun rose on the next day, The Butcher of Belfast emerged.

As the weeks passed, Darren grew to dislike the name of Butch, by which he was now addressed, but he couldn't deny the respect with which it was spoken. The legend grew around him and he heard how he had systematically removed each finger from the tortured man's hand. Darren really didn't think he'd done that, but he couldn't honestly remember. The whole incident seemed unreal to him, as if he had dreamed it, but the Spaniard was there to remind him that it was all true.

Although he never found out his real name, Darren grew to like the man, even learning some Spanish, and was sorry when he finally had to leave.

'I have some gifts for you,' said his new friend on their last day together.

Darren accepted the book, "Speak Spanish in a month", with a grateful smile, but his eyes widened at the second offering. A valuable antique, it had been lovingly fashioned by craftsmen a hundred years or so ago. It was an incredibly mean and savage looking switchblade, six inches long, slim, flat and heavy, with brass fittings at each end of the polished hardwood handle. In the centre of the wood a row of raised brass letters spelled out the word *Matador.* He was impressed with the gift, but also confused. 'What has this to do with bullfighting?' he asked.

The Spaniard's lips curled upwards forming a nasty and intimidating smile as he answered him. 'Nothing, my friend. *Matador* is simply Spanish word, which means *Killer.* The word, it is used in bullfighting, yes, but that is just because the fighter, he *kills* the bull.' For a moment longer he fingered the weapon, as lovingly as he would a fine woman, then handed it over. 'And you are a good killer, Mr. Butch. I think you are the best killer I ever see.'

Darren took the knife in his hand. It felt good and, when he pushed the brass release button, he couldn't help but grin to himself as the razor-like blade flew out of the side. He fell instantly in love with the knife. From the sight of the action to the hissing sound the blade made as it shot out, it seemed they were made for each other. This switchblade, *The Killer,* had been carried always, and used to wonderful effect ever since.

4

The Execution, 1981

Darren stood at the crumbling red brick doorway and took a quick breath of the cold, damp morning air. A quick, cautious glance had to suffice as surveillance and satisfy him that nobody was watching. Gently he pushed open the dilapidated, rotten and creaking door. Thankfully everything was quiet, just as he expected. A final check and still nothing moved. He was inside in a flash, closing the door behind him as quickly and silently as possible.

Once through the door, he froze. He stood still as a statue and held his breath as he waited and listened. Not a sound was to be heard from inside the rundown little terrace house. This dwelling was perfectly positioned, as it stood close to the corner junction of Springfield Road and the Falls Road. Breathing a little easier now he slowly, and deliberately, began creeping upstairs in the fashion of an old tomcat silently stalking his next meal.

The instant he reached the top step he stopped dead in his tracks, barely daring to breathe as a high-pitched squeal screamed through his ears. Momentarily he froze, then continued on his way as he realised the sound was only the donkey's years old floorboards as they rubbed together, protesting their annoyance against the intrusion of his weight. 'Jesus, Mary mother of God,' he whispered under his breath, quickly crossing himself. Reaching the landing at the top of the stairs he rapidly made his way to the front bedroom. Once there he slunk down as low as possible and crawled along until he arrived at the broken old sash-window seconds later.

Lifting his head a tad he risked a quick, sly peek through the centre of the dirty broken windowpane. As he gazed along the seemingly endless rows of dilapidated old terrace houses he had a prime view of the intricate artwork each one proudly exhibited. Most of the houses and buildings had their own mural boldly painted on one of their walls, and in glorious Technicolor too, for all to see. These were actual portraits, works of art, not the tatty graffiti usually seen in the inner cities of the UK. They were brightly coloured masterpieces depicting the evergreen scenes of *The Irish Tricolour, I.R.A. Sniper at work* and, of course, the all time favourite stating simply, *Brits out.*

All was calm on the street with just a few women who, as usual, were standing around gossiping with friends and neighbours. There was also the obligatory gang of kids playing on their bikes, fighting and generally looking for mischief. A quick glance at his watch confirmed that he still had around seven minutes left to wait, so he leaned on the cold and damp bedroom wall and lit a Capstan full strength cigarette, inhaling deeply. Sitting, smoking and waiting, he began to calm himself, caressing his crucifix and, as was his ritual, saying a few prayers too. He was pretty sure God was on their side, and now seemed a good enough time to pray.

He stubbed out his cigarette and reached across to the loose floorboard. It gave way easily. A moment later he pulled out a long, thin package that had been wrapped in a sheet of old Hessian sacking. Unwrapping the cloth from the *Widowmaker,* the Provos nickname given to the Armalite AR-18 assault rifle, his next few moments were spent cleaning and checking out the weapon's action and its twenty-round mag. He smiled to himself as he found it had been well cleaned and oiled recently. It was absolutely perfect, as was the scope and its mount.

He started to recite yet another prayer, but this one was not for him. It was for the thousands and thousands of Americans who, it seemed, worked all week long and then quite happily threw many of their hard earned Dollars into the buckets, which were passed around bars and pubs on a weekly basis. They gave quite readily to "the cause". This brand new, but not very shiny, Armalite AR-18 assault rifle had, of course, been sourced, bought, shipped and distributed by the all-important Yankee Dollar.

Prayers now done and finished, he pulled on his black woollen ski mask to cover every part of his head and face, with the exception of three holes, two for his eyes and one for his mouth. Adjusting the fit of the mask, then checking the rifle once more, he was ready. Quickly, he risked another peek through the broken windowpane. Nothing new was happening: the street was still quiet. Checking his watch again he muttered angrily, 'Shit, they're late, where the fuck are they?'

A few moments later, he clearly heard someone shouting. 'My name is Colonel McGuire, I am the acting commander of the 14th regiment of the Provisional I.R.A. Falls Road, Belfast.'

As Darren watched, five men came into his view. The bare-faced leader, he assumed, was the self-proclaimed Colonel McGuire while the other four Provos were typically dressed in camouflage uniforms and wearing the same woolly ski masks as Darren. Three of them were also carrying the evergreen Kalashnikov AK 47 assault rifles. Though these weapons had been adopted into service by the Soviet military as far back as 1949, they were still the weapon of choice by terrorist units worldwide, including the Provisional I.R.A. The AK's were proudly carried, and could be clearly seen by everyone there, as the group of men marched out into the middle of the street. Two of the Provos were dragging behind them another man; this man was not in uniform. He was kicking and screaming in protest, but he was dragged along nonetheless.

As the group gathered in the middle of the road the man who was dressed in "civvies" was forced to his knees, weeping and wailing all the time as he was pushed down. The Colonel made another announcement. 'Declan O'Brien, you have been found guilty of collaborating with the enemy. As an informer you have received the sentence of death with a public execution. Have you anything to say?'

The poor guy couldn't say a word; the only sounds heard were ones of weeping and heartbreak. A large crowd of men, women and kids had gathered by now. They were watching the execution squad with mounting interest and excitement. Darren could hear the constant chanting as it grew louder and louder. "Kill the traitor". "Shoot the bastard".

McGuire walked slowly and deliberately behind Declan. He reached down to his holster and unfastened the flap. Sliding out a black Colt .45 automatic pistol he chambered a round and placed the muzzle against the back of Declan's head.

'May God have mercy on your soul,' he intoned, then added in a whisper, 'you treacherous bastard,' as he pulled the trigger.

A loud crack was heard as the pistol fired. It echoed through the streets as Declan's head and face exploded with blood, brains and pieces of shattered skull flying in all directions. Cheers went up from the crowd. Gangs of women were laughing out loud as they walked closer, hurling insults and spitting on his still twitching body. Small kids were pushed forward and made to watch the gory scene. As usual they were told, 'this is what happens to informers. Don't forget what you've seen today kids. Now off you go and play like good boys and girls.'

Darren sat watching and smiled to himself. 'Serves the fucking idiot right,' he whispered as he pulled out another fag. Just as he was about to light it he heard the sound of approaching sirens. Placing the un-lit cigarette back into the pack, he waited. The crowd scattered and ran for shelter as the British Army Land Rover screeched to a halt, sirens still blazing, parking directly in front of the deceased, and now quite still, body of one Declan O'Brien. The next instant, doors flew open and the soldiers spewed out. They were instantly spread, down on one knee, with their rifles aimed in all directions.

One of the soldiers crept slowly up to the body to check for any sign of life. Feeling for a pulse and finding none, he looked back towards his unit. 'He's a dead un, sir,' the soldier shouted.

As the corpse was being checked, Darren was watching, carefully picking out his target. He'd quickly settled on the Sergeant. 'Fuckin' perfect, you'll do nicely you British bastard,' he grinned as he lifted the Armalite, taking aim at the soldier's stomach. It was always far better to shoot them in the guts. They would die eventually, but their prolonged screams of agony seemed to really unsettle the rest of the squad.

Still smiling, as he looked through the telescopic sights, Darren closely examined his target's face. He seemed to be around thirty-five years old and, even though he had one of those stupid British handlebar type moustaches, it was a hard face, the face of experience. A killer's face for sure, if ever he'd seen one. 'I wonder how many of our boys you've shot down in your time, you old bastard.' He slowly started to squeeze the trigger. Then he stopped dead, his finger coming away from the trigger as though it were electrified.

Victor was about as excited as any new squaddie could possible be. It was only the second week of his first tour here in Ulster, and already he was on an active patrol. He'd been impatiently waiting for just this moment ever since he'd joined up. 'Just wait until I'm back home on leave,' he grinned. 'I'll be a fucking hero. The fucking birds'll love me to bits.' He was quietly laughing to himself as he jumped out of the Land Rover.

'Oh no, no, no, not you, you old bastard,' Darren silently informed the Sergeant to whom he'd just granted the gift of life. With a wicked smirk crossing his face, Darren's mind raced as he focused on his new, far better, target. This one looked like a kid. 'A fuckin' boy soldier,' he smiled, as he retargeted. 'Bet you haven't even started shaving yet you little shit, have you?'

He zeroed in, inspecting the youth's happy looking face. 'I bet all these fuckers look after you, think of you as a son, the baby of the outfit, eh?' With that thought he lowered his aim down from the face and towards the young soldier's belly, whispering a final prayer. 'Forgive me Father, for I am about to sin. Please have mercy on his soul.'

The single shot rang out. As the young soldier fell backwards, a dark red circle replaced the random greens and browns of his camouflage jacket and he looked down in fascinated horror as it spread rapidly across his mid-section. He lay screaming in shock and pain, his hands instinctively reaching down, pressing on the wound. The pressure produced a plume of bright red blood, squirting upwards like a fountain, spraying the life-blood from his torn and ruptured young stomach.

***

At the very moment Darren pulled the trigger a foghorn sounded, but this haunting wail was not heard in Ireland. It was far away on a waterfront, in the great city of New York. It echoed around the ships and superstructures and wharf-sides, continuing off well into the distance. Jeff looked up from his desk, momentarily ignoring the immense pile of Dollar bills in front of him. A ship was entering port. He sat and watched it.

'C'mon buddy, we've work to do, and it won't get done with you staring out of the god damn window,' Ryan snapped.

'OK, OK, relax will ya. I was only taking a minute,' Jeff replied as he turned again to his pile.

Pushing a button he watched as another neat stack of bills was shrink-wrapped and automatically labelled. Placing this batch on top of the rest gave him a full pallet. He hit a different button, which now shrink-wrapped the entire pallet and its contents to form one thick, giant black plastic parcel. Jeff pressed the button on his mike. 'Another's ready,' he said in a bored, flat tone.

He yawned and stretched, lazily watching as the forklift driver collected the parcel and took it away towards the loading ramp. 'Holy shit, this is never ending,' he mumbled, yawning yet again. He still had another three hours left to go, counting and wrapping money, oiling and sealing pistols and rifles at the New York office of the infamous registered charity NORAID. Ryan McKee was in control of this, the Manhattan branch. An American by birth, but an Irishman at heart, McKee was a hard-line I.R.A. supporter.

***

Back in Belfast someone screamed out, 'Fuckin' 'ell, Stan. Stan, it's Vic. They got him. They got the kid in the fuckin' guts.'

The street had turned to complete chaos as Vic lay sprawled out on his back. His screams were an awful sound to hear as he cried, bled and very slowly died, right in front of his mates. They could do nothing but hunt and find the murdering Paddy bastard who'd shot him.

Darren moved fast, quickly fingering the selector switch. The instant he found "auto", he emptied the mag completely. Hot shell casings flew everywhere as he sprayed the street below with automatic gunfire. The sound of ricocheting bullets still echoing in his ears, he hurriedly rewrapped the sacking around the hot rifle and, after sliding it back under the floorboards, he quickly wiped dust around the area to cover the hiding place. Stopping only to pocket his fags and pull out his pistol he ran, gun in hand, downstairs, through the old door and into the street. A quick glance confirmed he was alone; there was no movement at all - until the front door of the house opposite swung slowly open.

An old lady stood in the doorway of her terrace house. Frowning in his direction she slowly shook her head, subconsciously stroking her blindingly white hair as she gave him the negative signal. Then, after taking another quick look to her left and right, her frown was replaced with a warm and gummy smile. She beckoned him towards her using her crooked, arthritic old finger in a "come here" manner. Smiling even more now, she blessed him as he left his doorway and shot through hers. As the door slammed shut with a bang, she shouted, 'God bless you son,' as he ran past her and straight through her house.

He continued on, running into the next home and the next. Three houses later he found he was alone in a small, cobble-stoned back alley. Turning to his left he could plainly hear the distinctive popping sound of several AK's as they fired repeatedly. He began running once more in the direction of the Kalashnikov rifles and the boys who were firing them. Though now out of breath, he struggled onward, down towards the main road and the friendly sound of the automatic gunfire.

Edward "Eddie" McQuillan was an intelligent man. A graduate of the Queen's University here in Belfast, and also of the University of Ulster, he had risen quickly through the ranks under the Accelerated Promotion System. He also proudly held the RUC Service Medal and had been commended on a number of occasions for the performance of his duty. Having served in most parts of Northern Ireland, including south Londonderry, Portadown, Crossmaglen, West Belfast, Holywood and Musgrave Street in Belfast city centre, he was no stranger to violence. He'd seen it all. He also hated the I.R.A. and its members with a vengeance.

When Sergeant McQuillan heard the pattern of fire – pistol shot, rifle shot, automatic rounds – an immediate scene formed in his head and he knew there was a sniper at work. He ran in the opposite direction from the noise. He was far too long in the tooth to run towards it. He knew from long experience that the instant a gunman had finished his work he would run like hell *away* from the area. After all, a sniper who stayed around to admire his work was, or would shortly be, a very dead sniper. McQuillan ran for around half a mile, then slowed.

Carefully he looked down the small back streets, one at a time, which led towards the hot area. He saw nothing. Street after street he checked without results. Then, as he was about to give up and return to the hot spot, he heard hurried footsteps coming in his direction. He tapped his service weapon three times before removing it from his belt, he liked threes, then he stood patiently at the junction of a small back street and the main road, waiting and holding his breath. Judging his moment carefully, he jumped out with the intention of blocking the runner's path, but he mistimed his appearance slightly. The runner was actually on top of him instead of the few feet away that he'd anticipated. The running man crashed heavily into him and the collision knocked the pair of them to the ground.

The point of impact was so hard and unexpected that Darren's pistol flew from his hand, while McQuillan landed heavily on a grate and his own weapon disappeared into the sewer system. The crash stunned the pair of them. Both dazed and winded they rolled about, gasping for breath, on the cobbled floor. McQuillan's eyes eventually began to refocus and he noticed the pistol lying about five feet away from him. Turning to face the runner a quick look of recognition flashed across his face.

'McCann, you murdering Catholic bastard,' he yelled, reacting instinctively and reaching inside his raincoat, desperately grasping for the Beretta, his secondary piece.

Still shocked by the savage impact, Darren was on his knees, a look of horror spreading across his face. 'Oh, Christ, not you, you bastard,' he shouted, staring at the Sergeant's face. Seeing the policeman's hand sliding under the coat, Darren knew he was going for a gun. He also realised he had no time to reach his own pistol. Using every ounce of his strength, he pulled up his head and sent it crashing down, directly into the stunned policeman's face.

The cop's eyes rolled upward as McCann's forehead smashed into his nose. Quickly Darren head-butted him again and again until the cop was obviously down and out. Rising quickly to his feet he stared for a second at the prostrate form of this much hated RUC man. Then, with a quick and violent swing of his boot, he kicked him with all the force he could muster, aiming straight into his face. As Darren's boot made contact, the cop's left eye socket smashed leaving the area around his eyebrow concave, his face changed forever to a bizarre appearance. The savage impact of the kick had forced his eyeball from its socket. It hung, crushed into a bloody pulp, as a mixture of blood and dark red jelly slowly oozed down his cheek.

Darren reached once more for his pistol, grabbed it and, hearing small arms fire coming from Brit guns, he knew they were very close by. He had no time to finish the man off now, so he turned and started running again. Within five minutes he was there inside the safe house. Quickly he closed the door behind him, breathing deeply as he locked it. He sat and waited.

As day turned into night the eerie shadows began to creep across the dusty floorboards towards him. Though he knew they were cast by the street lamp opposite, an involuntary shiver ran down Darren's spine as he watched. Sitting silently, the wait continued. He had nothing to eat and only water from the old decaying tap to drink. Still not daring to set foot outside, he had little option but to sit patiently and wait some more. Two days after the shooting, Darren was still sitting in the same spot, leaning against the cold, cracked tiles of the old fireplace. His eyes were starting to droop once more as he was at the point of drifting off to sleep again, but he jumped as he heard a noise. Forcing himself awake he opened his eyes wide. It was there again, he was sure. He could faintly hear a slight scratching - *and* it was coming from the door.

Darren took a deep breath and held it tightly in his chest. Trembling, he stood behind the door, straining his ears as he listened. The old worn out hinges creaked and groaned as it slowly swung wider and wider, until at last it was fully open. He could clearly hear the rain gently falling outside now as he waited, motionless, behind the open door. Slowly he began easing out his pistol. 'Too loud,' he realised, as he slid it back into his belt. His hand reached, inch by inch, for *The Killer.* Sliding it from his pocket he felt instantly reassured. That familiar feel, the mix of cold brass and warm wood, was good in his grip. It was like shaking hands with an old and trusted friend. Slitting his eyes in an attempt to gain a little better night vision, he watched as the shadow of a single figure was cast on the floor. The shadow then took a slow and deliberate footstep forwards, making it seem altogether bigger and more intimidating as it grew in the room. The next step taken caused a piece of gravel to crunch as it was flattened and crushed underfoot. Darren pushed the button at the same instant. The blade sprang out and locked into place as if it were a living thing, the snap of its action concealed perfectly by the sound of the shadowy footstep.

Though the night was cold and damp, a constant trickle of sweat dripped down his face as the shadow grew in size, the extra steps sharpening the edges to the clear silhouette of a man. Once inside, the man gingerly pushed the door behind him. It creaked as it closed and then, once more, there was nothing but silence. Darren gripped *The Killer* hard. Springing forward he grabbed the man from behind and held him tightly around the throat. Hand raised, he prepared for the kill; a quick thrust to the heart was swift, effective and deadly, but best of all, it was silent.

'Butch, Butch... it's me, Thomas... for fuck's sake... let me go... you mad cunt,' the man croaked between gasps of much needed air. Darren slowly released his arm lock and spun the man around. He stood facing him, still with *The Killer* poised, but after only a second's inspection he was convinced that the man he was about to kill really was his long time friend and comrade Thomas Mallone.

'Are you fucking crazy Thomas? You don't just walk in on someone like that.' Tutting in Thomas's direction, he spat, 'Have you never heard of knocking man? And maybe saying something like... it's me, Thomas, please don't stick me with that big fuck off knife of yours - thank you very much.' Then, in a sarcastic tone he told him, 'I should have stabbed you in the friggin' arse, just for being stupid.'

Thomas, normally a man of few words, except when he was with his old mate Butch, gave him one of his famous "looks", which basically said, "bollocks to you!" 'Oh aye, that'd look fuckin' wonderful wouldn't it? And here's meself knocking on the door of a fuckin' derelict house shouting out at the top of me voice. Hello, I'm here to see the sniper who killed two Brits the other day. Oh aye and by the way, would you be needing a bit of dinner?'

'Two of 'em?' Darren was shocked. 'Must've been a lucky shot when I emptied the mag.'

'Aye, and another one in hospital. In critical condition too, that one is.'

'Fuck me, I never expected that.' Darren looked his friend up and down before asking impatiently, 'what have you brought me? You said something about dinner, where is it? And what is it? I'm fucking starving to death here man.'

'Ham sarnies son, here you go.' Thomas grinned as he tossed over a greasy, brown paper bag. 'Sorry I couldn't get here any sooner, but the place has been fuckin' crawling with Brits.

I've never ever seen so many of the bastards in all me life.'

Darren snatched the bag and, smiling with satisfaction, ripped it open. Sighing contentedly he quickly wolfed down the sandwiches. Finishing the last one he sat licking his lips. 'Jesus, they were good... So, what's the news then?' he asked excitedly.

'You're as hot as they come mate. They've issued a "wanted" for you, *and* it's got your fucking photo on it too. Been plastered everywhere it has,' Thomas replied. 'The word is, you've been called down to Cross me old son. And from there, they're gonna fuck you off someplace else - until things quiet down a bit.' They chatted a little longer until Thomas stood to leave, explaining, 'Got to go to sort some stuff out for you Butch me old mate.'

When he returned around three hours later, Thomas whispered, 'It's me, put that fucking great dagger down will ya?' *before* he poked his head round the open door.

Darren stood giggling like a schoolgirl at the sight of his friend, who was nervously peering into the darkened room. 'I'm over here, you bog Irish cunt,' he whispered in the direction of the door.

'Well I still can't see a fucking thing, it's pitch black in here, and I'm not too sure if I want to cast me eyes on a fucking *Englishman* anyhow,' Thomas replied in a mocking tone. As Darren had been born and raised in Belfast, part of a British colony, he held a British, *not Irish,* passport. And Thomas would never miss an opportunity to remind him of this fact.

'Fuck you, and fuck your passport too,' Darren snapped.

'Always gets a rise, never fails,' Thomas thought to himself, as he gleefully grinned in the direction of the voice. 'Come on Butch, I'm to take you out to collect your transport, so get yer stuff together will you.'

Making their way out of the building the pair of them stood in the darkened doorway and, after a moment or two spent checking that the coast was clear, they sneaked off into the dead of night. Darren followed closely on his friend's heels as they headed towards a brilliant-white Transit van with "Big Jack's Frozen Pies" painted on the side in red day-glo letters a foot high.

'Christ all-fucking-mighty, I'm glad you came in something that blends in - we wouldn't be wanting to be standing out or anything, now would we?'

'It's fine; stop your moaning will you. You're like an old woman,' Thomas complained and then laced his voice with sarcasm as he asked, 'are all Englishmen the same?' Darren said nothing; he just glared back at Thomas. These bleedin' English jokes were really starting to piss him off.

Out of town they drove, heading towards the small settlement of Hillsborough. Eventually Thomas pulled the Transit into a deserted lay-by, which was just on the outskirts of the town. As they stopped and parked, Darren noticed that they were sitting directly behind a battered, old and badly brush-painted Ford Escort van. Thomas glanced across to his mate with a smile on his face and announced, 'There she is me old son, and a beautiful little runner she is too - only one little old lady owner, used it purely for going to church on Sundays.' Then, with an even bigger grin, he added, 'Honest!'

Climbing out of "the pie van", Darren inspected his "new" transport, and sighed. 'Holy fuck.'

'Aye,' said Thomas as he held out his hand. Darren took it, shook it warmly, and they said their goodbyes. Opening the rusted door he climbed into the old Ford. It sputtered and coughed as he turned the key but, miraculously, started first time. Driving off in a south-westerly direction, the van slowly disappeared into the night through a haze of blue exhaust smoke.

Despite the intense presence of the security forces in Belfast itself, the county roads heading out of the city were very quiet; so quiet in fact that Darren saw hardly any other traffic at all. Driving for around twenty minutes he had seen only six other vehicles, and two of those had been delivery trucks. He slowed a little as he approached the turn-off leading to the infamous Republican stronghold of Crossmaglen. Reducing his speed even more he turned down the small lane and began to relax. He was finally in prime "Bandit Country".

'There, I'm much safer now,' he said aloud, as the "Bandits" living around here were his own special breed of people; comrades, brothers in arms and, most of all, trusted friends.

As the van slowly rattled down the tree-lined, leafy, single-track lane he passed the orange, white and green letters brazenly spelling out I.R.A. Each letter was around three feet tall and fastened to a telegraph pole. They proudly announced the boundary of the village of "Cross" itself. Just below the I.R.A. sign there was another. This one was similar to the "men at work" sign seen on roads and motorways everywhere but, instead of a man shovelling, it had the silhouette of a man with a rifle with the words "sniper at work" written underneath. He smiled to himself, amused by the obvious disregard of British authority here. Continuing down the lane, he noticed a light in the distance. A lamp was being swung, deliberately, from side to side. Slowing even more now, he cautiously approached the light. Though now travelling only at walking speed, he put the van into first gear and was ready to accelerate away in an instant should the need arise.

A single man stood in the centre of the road, his hand in the air signalling to Darren to stop. Following the man's instruction he came to a halt at his side, then wound the window down in an effort to look the guy over. The old Ford remained in first gear, though, just in case. The dark figure who stood at the driver's side window slowly slid out an old-looking revolver, which he pointed directly at Darren's head as he barked the order, 'Get out of the van and keep your hands where I can see 'em,' quickly adding in a stern voice, 'and I'll be standing for no funny business; or any of yer hanky panky either.'

Doing as he was told, Darren got out of the van whilst trying his best to hide the smile he felt growing on his lips. The man stood with only the half-light of the moon at his back to illuminate him and let out a slow whistle. Seconds later two other men emerged from the bushes to join him.

'So, Sonny Jim, what are you doing driving around here on a dark night like tonight? Up to some no good monkey business, I'll be betting,' the guy asked him.

Glancing at the other two fellows, Darren saw they were armed too. One had another equally old-looking revolver and the other was carrying what appeared to be an actual Lee Enfield bolt-action rifle of the Victorian era.

'Fuck me, I'm about to be held up by Dick Turpin and co,' he smirked as he surveyed the three "Bandits", who looked for all the world as if they'd bought their weapons at an Antiques Roadshow discount arms auction.

'Do you know who we are?' asked the "outlaw" leader in a serious tone.

'No... I've no idea. Who are you?'

'Well Sonny Jim, we are the fucking I.R.A. and I'll bet you are absolutely shitting yourself - aren't you?'

'Do you have a radio with you?' Darren asked the leader.

'What?'

'I said, do you have a radio with you?'

'Of course I have, you idiot. I have to use a radio to keep in constant touch with headquarters,' the man explained importantly.

'Give it here then.'

'You... you can't have it, it's mine, and this field-radio is for official business, and to be used for incoming orders and my reports – only.'

'OK then, report this - if you don't mind, that is.' Darren then reeled off D.M.B.O.B.786, which the leader reluctantly repeated into the handset. The reply came back instantly. The leader, keeping a tight hold of his radio, but holding it to Darren's ear, could hear only one half of the call, which went something like this.

'Yes, yes it's me... I don't know... yes I am... they say they're the I.R.A - OK, I will.' Darren looked at the leader, telling him, 'He wants to speak to you.'

The man looked puzzled, but took the handset anyway. 'Hello, who is this speaking? Yes we have... but we were just... all right... OK... I mean, yes sir... I know, I'm... we're... right away sir, yes, I know, I'm sorry... I'm very sorry... I will, yes immediately sir.' With that he finished the call and stared at Darren for a moment. Then, eyes wide with incredulity, he stood rigidly to attention - and saluted him. His two compatriots, clearly clueless, followed his lead and did the same.

Darren slowly sauntered back towards the van past three very confused, saluting bandits. He opened the door, then turned back and faced them. As he did, he caught the last part of their low, whispered conversation, '... of fucking Belfast, that's fucking who!'

'The next time you three wankers are on patrol out here,' (Darren's voice was dripping with sarcasm as he used the word patrol) 'I suggest you first find out *exactly* who you're talking to - before you introduce yourselves... 'Cos if I'd been one of the Prods, all three of you stupid cunts would be as dead as doornails by now... Now, fuck off... Go and guard your sheep, or cows, or whatever else it is you spend all night shagging. Go on, fuck off I said. You're relieved.'

The three I.R.A. "terrorists" remained rigid as, slack jawed, they continued to stare at him. The man they had threatened at gunpoint only a few moments ago had now been magically transformed into the Devil himself. The eerie reflection of moonlight had seemingly given him a pair of terrible, white-glowing eyes.

'Go on, fuck off I said,' Darren snapped one last time. Guns and torch now dropped, they quickly disappeared into the bushes, and the blackness of the night. Chuckling to himself, Darren got back into the van, started the engine and drove off, once more in the inevitable cloud of blue exhaust smoke.

A short while later he was driving past a high, old red brick wall, which continued as far as he could see. Eventually, though, he noticed an elaborate gateway and sharply turned the steering wheel of the old Ford. As he pulled into the drive his mouth dropped at the sight of the big old country house. It looked so impressive that he could imagine Queen Elizabeth herself living in a place such as this. Continuing down the driveway he stopped at the front of the house, turned off the ignition and parked. Climbing out of the van he noticed a light come on at the impressive old arched stone doorway. The door opened and a smiling figure came out and stood waving to him. Darren hurriedly crossed the gravel drive and saluted the man.

'Ah don't be bothering with all that stuff Butch me lad. Come on in and get yourself a warm.' He led Darren by the arm, and continued through the hallway into a large living room, which had a lovely log and peat fire roaring merrily away. 'Come on, get a warm here lad,' said Willy, The Boss.

As he stood in the welcoming glow of the fire, Willy looked at him, 'You know, you really made a stupid mistake the other day lad, letting that piece of shite, McQuillan, get a close look at you.'

'Aye, I know that sir, but it couldn't be helped. It all happened too fast to do anything about it - and I knew the Brits were closing in on me. I just had to run - and leave the bastard alive.'

'I know, I know lad. I received a full report the next day. Oh yes, and by the way, that was good work too. You're a fine shot Butch lad, but the thing is, now your photo's to be seen everywhere. You'll have to lay low for a while. Do you understand?'

'Yes sir, I understand,' Darren replied.

'Well, I've organised a little trip for you, and you'll have to be gone for quite a while too. This isn't a punishment, though. I want you to understand that. It's just that if you stay here in Ireland - well, you'll end up in the Maze, and there's too many of our fine young lads in the H-Blocks already. So it's for your own sake, are you sure you understand that?'

'Yes sir, I do understand fully,' he nodded.

'Good lad, now Mary's got a nice stew prepared for you.' Willy passed him a small envelope telling him, 'and here's your orders. You're to head south after your meal, and only open them when you're well away from here, OK?'

Saluting again he replied, 'Yes sir, and thank you sir.'

A couple of hours later and Darren was fit to burst. He'd crammed in as much of that beautiful stew as he could, for he didn't know for sure when he would next be able to eat. Waving goodbye to the Boss, he climbed back into the old Ford, turned the ignition key and the engine came to life. OK, so there was another cloud of smoke accompanying the initial start, but it had started, and it had started every single time, first time, every time. He was actually getting to like driving around in the old rust bucket. It was reliable after all, even if it did look a little ropey. As he drove along on the Dublin road he spotted a likely looking lay-by. It seemed quiet enough and was in darkness as there were no street-lamps. So, just before the town of Drogheda, he pulled in and, setting the handbrake, he parked up. Flicking the interior light on as he opened the envelope, he scowled as he read the instructions. He was more than a little disappointed to find that he had been ordered to report to a haulage company down in Cork.

'Shite, that means I'm being sent across to Europe - France or bleedin' Belgium most likely. Jesus, hope it's not for long,' he sat and muttered to himself.

Then, after taking a quick pee in the bush, he was off again heading down south, but this time he had a destination - "A&R Transport, Kinsale, county Cork."

5

The Englishman

Anthony was simply known as "The Englishman" by the majority of Dublin's locals. He was a very quiet, private and sad-looking man who, though only forty-seven, appeared considerably older than his years. Passing his fellow shopkeepers he offered a polite "good morning" to each of them. No one really knew that much about him, with the exception that he was English and quiet, but most of all he seemed very lonely. He was neither liked nor disliked by anyone, including the hard line republicans who, though they hated the Brits with a passion, simply tolerated this pathetic old man.

He arrived at the door to his little antique shop and entered to the familiar musty smell of old furniture, paintings and clothing. He flipped the sign, which hung on the glass door, from closed to open as he turned on the lights. Walking to the back of his shop he went through to his office, turned the kettle on and prepared his tea. This small room had a window from which he could see anyone entering his shop.

The tea sat steaming on his desk as he packed and lit his pipe. Puffing away he sat and waited for today's buyers. His clients were mainly American tourists who delighted in "discovering" the small shop, which stood at the far end of a small alley and was practically hidden from view, just off Cope Street. The Americans seemed to love the Temple Bar district of Dublin and couldn't get enough "genuine antiques from the old country", which they happily bought and shipped back to the States, seemingly by the ton. Sipping his tea Anthony glanced up to his wall clock. Though he always tried to avoid being alone at this particular time, today he had arrived early. It was 8.35 and, as he stared at the clock's face, a single teardrop began rolling slowly down his cheek and he was unable to prevent his thoughts taking him back to that awful morning, almost twenty years ago.

It was the second day of his honeymoon and he had woken to find he was alone in bed, his new bride already up and about somewhere. 'Hello and a good morning to you, sweetheart,' he sang aloud, but there was no answer. Quickly dressing, he searched their rooms and found the bathroom door locked. 'Oh,' he remembered whispering. As a newly married man he was now fully aware of a lady's need for privacy in the morning. 'Looks like I'll be making breakfast today.'

He wasn't sure how long he should wait, but as breakfast began to grow cold he was starting to worry. He returned to the bathroom where his gentle knocking on the door quickly changed to frantic hammering. Eventually he was forced to break open the door, and there he found her. His beloved Katherine lay dead on the floor, a small pool of blood soaking her long, blonde hair. The doctor later informed him that it seemed she had slipped whilst getting out of the bath. Having banged her head on the tiled floor, she'd suffered a 'traumatic head injury'. This wasn't uncommon and was, 'just one of those things I'm afraid,' he remembered the faceless doctor explaining.

Wiping away the tear he forced his gaze away from the clock and back to the desk. 'Pull yourself together you old fool. You have the shop, and you have your work,' Anthony sighed as he removed a sheaf of documents from his safe. The five envelopes he picked out looked identical. The only differences were the handwritten amounts marked on each of them. He selected the one with £75 in the top right-hand corner and slid it inside the Irish Times newspaper. He returned the others to the safe and locked it. Glancing down at the underside of the desktop he removed the double-barrelled sawn-off shotgun from its cradle, which was aimed directly at the seat opposite his own chair. Changing the shells for fresh ones, he cocked both hammers and replaced the gun in the mounting. His tea was clap cold and he checked the clock again. 11.50. 'Where on earth does the time go?' he mumbled as he took his favourite handgun, a Smith and Wesson .38 revolver, from his drawer and, after checking its ammunition, pocketed the pistol. An automatic gun remained in the drawer. The extra bullets it held were useful at times, but Turner preferred to trust his safety to the good, old-fashioned mechanism of the .38.

Leaving the shop, he flipped the sign to read "closed", then strolled slowly down the road. He arrived at Ashton Quay and took his usual place on the bench, lighting his pipe as he gazed silently over the river. The view brought him a contentment he needed and relished.

'Morning Mr. Turner,' the man said, announcing his presence.

'Good morning to you too young fellow,' Anthony replied. 'What do you have for me?' he enquired, as he pushed the newspaper along the bench.

The young man shuffled closer as he whispered, 'That shooting up in Belfast, you know the Springfield and Falls Road one, it was the I.R.A. who shot the informer.'

Anthony held up his hand to stop him. Staring at him he snapped, 'McCartney, do you genuinely expect Her Majesty to pay you good money for supplying information that everyone in the province is fully aware of? Good God old chap, what on earth are you thinking?'

'No, no, not the bit about *that* shooting; it's about the shooting that followed. You know, when the soldiers were killed. I know who the shooter was,' he explained in an even quieter tone, before continuing, 'and I know where he's heading.'

McCartney told Anthony Turner every detail he knew about this latest atrocity.

When he'd finished he took the newspaper, along with the cash in the envelope, and walked away, quickly losing himself in the Dublin crowds. As he watched the man disappear, Anthony re-lit his pipe and sat a few minutes longer. Eventually he stood, smoothed his overcoat and sauntered off in the direction of his shop. This new information was important; it needed reporting urgently, but he also knew that to be seen rushing along the streets of Dublin could get him noticed, possibly by the wrong people. He was never, ever noticed. He blended in. Every day he did the same thing - sell antiques and walk slowly to and from the shop. That was his life here in Dublin. Though he hadn't worn the uniform for almost twenty years (since the death of his wife he had preferred to work alone) his S.A.S training still remained. He *was* the quiet, slightly eccentric and infirm antique shop owner. He was *not* the handler of paid informants. To loose sight of this simple fact could, and in all probability would, result in the loss of his life.

6

The Trip from Hell

About halfway down to Cork Darren stopped, pulling the old van into the car park of a quaint little thatched pub. There he had a tasty steak pie for lunch, and washed it down with a lovely pint of Murphy's stout. Back on the road again, and soon he was almost in Cork. Following the directions he'd been given, he turned off to the left and was now heading out in the general direction of the quaint old seaside town of Kinsale. Just before he reached it he saw some large white buildings on his right. Then he spotted a sign announcing in giant blue letters, "A&R Transport and Haulage, daily service to England, Ireland and Europe". He pulled in and parked on the forecourt in front of the main building. Leaving the keys in the van, he walked straight into the office and told the girl on reception, 'Hello, my name's Fitzpatrick, I'm here to see a Mr. Elliott.'

'One moment please Mr. Fitzpatrick. Take a chair, and I'll see if he's available,' she told him in her lovely soft country accent, which sounded to him more like she was singing than talking.

He took a seat in the corner and waited. Within five minutes the office door opened and a very fat, short, balding man came through. He looked at Darren and said in an unmistakable southern English voice, 'Good morning Mr. Fitzpatrick, how are you today? I'm Philip, the owner. Would you like to come through to the office?' As they walked by he asked Tuila, the pretty secretary with the beautiful accent, to bring them in tea and biscuits.

They sat chatting about how terrible the troubles were, the long drive from the North, the weather, and the transport business, of which Darren knew absolutely nothing. Moments later, the lovely Tuila knocked and entered carrying a tray, on which was a pot of steaming hot tea, plus a good selection of homemade biscuits. She set the tray down, turned and smiled at him, then left.

The instant the door closed behind her Philip leaned over the desk, whispering to Darren that he had that very morning received orders to take him across to Northern Spain. 'Oh, and don't let the accent bother you too much,' he explained. 'Though I was raised in Surrey, England, I'm as Irish as you are. My parents were originally from Waterford. My dad moved us all over to the UK for work years ago, when I was still a baby.' Hearing this, Darren gave an audible sigh of relief. He suddenly felt safe again as he was back with his own kind - regardless of the accent. 'You'll stay with us tonight and be on my lad's truck at 7am, bound for sunny Spain. I think you'll like it too. Must be warmer than here, eh?'

Early the next morning, after taking a large fried breakfast, Darren stood and shivered as he waited in the cold, clammy morning air. Looking up at the huge Seddon Atkinson articulated lorry he wondered where, exactly, he would be riding, as it was obviously already fully loaded with forty-five gallon oil drums. Philip came walking towards him with another man whom he introduced as Steve, his eldest son. The two men shook hands.

'Steve will be driving you,' Philip told him, 'but, you surely can't ride up front.

You're much too hot for that. Unfortunately you are going to have to travel in the hide.'

Darren watched in dismay as the father and son started to unscrew the end of one of the oil drums, which was on the bottom row halfway down the trailer. As he looked inside, he discovered that three drums had been welded together especially for the job of concealing contraband. Darren was well aware of this kind of hiding place, but he'd never imagined himself inside one. It looked like a long pipe and the air holes drilled in the top, he assumed, were especially for him.

'Jesus, I'll be like a rat in a sewer,' he said quietly.

Philip heard the comment and turned to face Darren. 'Maybe so, but you'll be out of the "sewer" in a couple of days. Our boys in the H-blocks won't be nearly so lucky.'

Darren nodded his head feeling deeply ashamed of himself. After all, how could he possibly complain at a couple of days cooped up in there when his brothers were locked in Long Kesh and would be there for years and years to come? He crept cautiously on hands and knees into the elongated oil drum and, at the far end, found an old worn sleeping bag that would serve as his bed, plus what looked like a bedpan. Oh joy. There was just enough headroom for him to sit in a hunched position and he put the two water containers Philip had given him at the opposite end of the drum, then his loaf of bread and lump of cheese next to his bed. Philip leaned in and wished him good luck, then waved farewell as he and Steve picked up the drum top and slowly screwed it down tight. Inside it went pitch black - he couldn't see a thing. He almost panicked in the first few minutes, but eventually managed to calm himself.

The huge diesel engine quickly turned over and fired into life. He could feel every single one of the vibrations from the engine's slow revolutions as it sat smoothly ticking over. Next he was aware of voices. He recognised one as belonging to Philip, as he bade goodbye to his son. Then the vibrations sped up and, accelerating away, they were off.

Darren assumed they would be going to the Cork ferry, and then on to Spain. Though there was no event to break the monotony of the journey, to call it uneventful would have been a downright and dirty lie - a very dirty lie. He was violently sick, constantly throwing up until his stomach cramped owing to the vomit inducing motion of a very rough ferry crossing. One particularly turbulent wave threw his "toilet" in the air, and that was that. He coughed and spluttered as his own waste engulfed him. 'Dear God help me,' he screamed into the darkness.

He thought it must be his second day sealed up tight inside the drums, but really it could've been anywhere from one to ten days. He had lost all sense of time and couldn't have said how long it had been if you'd offered him all the Guinness in Ireland.

7

Euskal Herria AKA the Basque Country

The truck made two stops during the ferry ride from hell, but still he was not allowed out. The third time it stopped he heard a tapping on the far end where the empty bedpan had come to rest. He then faintly heard Steve's voice as he whispered, 'Won't be long now. Take it easy, you'll be out soon.'

'Jesus, and won't I look a sight?' he said under his breath. He was soaking wet from the foul mixture of piss, vomit and, worse, his own shit. As the vile potion had been mixed together it had swilled around his home due to the motion of the truck on the ferry. 'Oh bollocks,' he thought as he tried to inspect himself. 'I'm fucking wet through and covered in it. It's in my hair, beard, fucking everywhere.' Though he didn't realise it, he was moaning out loud now.

The noise at the toilet end had gone from a quiet tapping to a cringing high-pitched squeal, as Steve started unscrewing and removing the cap. The instant the cap came off an incredibly bright light assaulted his eyes as the Spanish sun invaded his home. Steve took an involuntary step back followed by three or four more as he quickly retreated, standing well out of the stench. He stood looking in, not daring to get too close, before calling out, 'Hey, are you OK in there?' On hands and knees Darren came slowly crawling out towards him. Steve retreated even farther. 'Holy shit, that fucking reeks to high Heaven. Are you sure you're all right? Smells like something's curled up and died,' he exclaimed, as he stood with a mixed look of disgust and revulsion on his face. Then the smile took over. He couldn't help it, but the sight of Darren's head poking out, dripping with slime and shit, seemed altogether too funny. He broke out laughing so hard that tears rolled down his face.

Darren jumped out and, despite making a nasty squelching sound as he hit the floor, stood and straightened his jacket and smoothed his trousers, doing his utmost to make himself look reasonably presentable. 'I'd like to see how you look and smell under similar circumstances,' he snapped in what he hoped was a defiant manner.

An old lady stood by watching the commotion. She was standing in front of three very thin farmer types. Looking down her nose, she tutted with an "I'm absolutely disgusted with you" air and pointed at a well-lit, blazing bonfire. Pulling an even more disapproving face she stood, constantly clasping and then releasing her hands, shouting at the top of her voice and looking upwards, as if to God, protesting violently about something. Darren couldn't understand a single word, but he did understand the authority with which she pointed a long, sharpened stick in his direction. Her head began to shake even more violently, and then she protested some more.

'Who's that old crow - and what the hell is she saying?' Darren asked Steve, who had to brave the smell and move closer to catch his words.

'That old crow,' Steve happily informed him, 'is the new woman in your life. She's the head of the family, and the absolute boss in these parts, and she's cursing you. She says that you not only look like a filthy animal, but you smell worse than any pig or cow she has ever seen in the whole of her seventy two years on Earth.' Steve carried on grinning as he translated further. 'Another thing, you have to strip off all of your clothes and throw them on her bonfire. Now, she says, as that's the only thing they're fit for.'

'Charmed, I'm sure.' Darren sulked and asked, 'Does the old hag say anything else?'

'As a matter of fact, yes, she does. She says the sea is that way.' He pointed for effect.

'Why the fuck would I be needing to know where the bleedin' sea is?'

'Because that's where you have to go and bathe, and because she won't let you anywhere near her house smelling like that,' Steve chuckled.

Hanging his head low Darren slowly stripped off his stinking rags. He handed Steve *The Killer* for safe keeping and, when he was completely naked, the old girl started raving again, pointing at the bonfire and then towards the sea. Even he didn't need that translating so he did as she ordered and, after tossing his stuff onto the fire, wandered off with what he hoped was a modicum of dignity, naked as a jaybird - in search of the sea.

Eventually, wandering along the small pathway, he arrived at a low cliff face. He climbed down and found himself standing in a small isolated bay with a rocky beach. Walking towards the water he gingerly waded in. It was bitterly cold and not at all what he had expected of sunny Mediterranean Spain, but he had to admit that it felt absolutely wonderful after his incarceration. He had a good scrub and, as he grew accustomed to the temperature, took a long swim to ease out the pains from his cramped body. Finally he moved to the water's edge where he dithered until he was dry.

Darren hurried back along the trail, his arms wrapped around himself in an effort to keep warm. Shivering as he went, he couldn't wait to get back to put on some nice warm clothes. Unfortunately for him, that wasn't going to happen immediately. He stood once more in front of the old girl, allowing her to inspect and approve of him - which she didn't. As she approached him, she sniffed the air, spat, and shook her head once more pointing across the yard.

'What the bloody hell is she pointing at now?' he wondered aloud. Poking him along with her stick she herded Darren into a small fenced area. Around twenty yards farther and he stopped dead in his tracks, his jaw falling open when he saw what faced him. 'Oh no, Jesus woman, no, no, no, you can't be serious. That's a - a fucking sheep dip!'

She pointed again then poked him with the sharpened stick and followed up with a well-aimed slap. He jumped as he felt the sting across his buttocks, but tried to remain defiant.

'Shite, no way am I getting in that. No fucking chance you old bitch,' he protested, but she kept prodding and slapping until he had to admit defeat and climb in. The dip seemed even colder than the sea.

A large, oblong block of carbolic soap hit him squarely on the forehead. The boss-lady's mood seemed to have improved as she stood tittering away, clearly pleased with her well-aimed shot and highly amused by the sight of him standing dithering in a sheep dip. Then the shouting started again. One minute she was congratulating herself on her perfect aim, and the next she was screaming what, he could only assume, meant 'wash, wash, wash!'

He scrubbed and scrubbed until he was certain, he knew for sure, beyond a shadow of a doubt, that he was finally, spotlessly, thoroughly clean. So, after a final rinse, he climbed out and waited once more for the old crow's approval. She sauntered over and began sniffing him again. She gave him a thorough inspection, lifting his arms and checking behind his ears. Then, though she continued gabbling on and on, she actually nodded and smiled. He could hardly believe it.

'Have I passed inspection now?' He looked across to Steve.

'Yep, and you can go into the house for a proper bath. She says so.'

The old lady cast her eye over Darren for a moment. Then, taking him by the hand as she would a child, she led him into the derelict-looking old farmhouse and up to her bathroom. She opened the door, whilst still holding his hand, and he stood rigid as his mouth dropped wide open. Staring into the room Darren was stunned. Here, in the middle of nowhere, in a rickety, old, seemingly falling to bits and dilapidated farmhouse, he was gazing on a bathroom fit for a king. It simply oozed luxury. The huge sunken oval bath was filled to the brim with steaming, foamy water. The floor was tiled with marble in an intricate pattern of wild flowers, and the fittings looked as if they might be real gold. Pushing him towards the bath, the old dear smiled again and said something else he couldn't work out. Then she handed him another bar of soap, which was a great improvement on having one thrown at him – and this one smelled nice too. She offered him a few more words in her very foreign voice, blew a quick kiss, winked and left.

He eased himself down into the scalding hot water. Sitting and relaxing in the sweet smelling bubble bath felt really good after being cooped up for so long. He closed his eyes and slowly ducked his head below the surface. When he came up again he sighed and started softly singing a few lines of "A Wild Colonial Boy." After his escape from the cold transport yard in Kinsale, a swim in the frigid sea and the freezing sheep dip, this bath felt like Heaven.

He had been soaking for around half an hour when a knock came to the door. Darren opened his eyes and shouted for the visitor to come in. The old girl was back again. She stood at the doorway with a huge white towel, a pile of clothes and a friendly smile on her wizened old face. She said something else he couldn't understand, put down the towel and clothes, and left again. He took a much-needed shave, doused himself in loads of fresh smelling deodorant and aftershave, dressed and left the bathroom.

He was out in the main hallway and he could hear voices. Following the sounds he eventually ended up at the doorway of a large dining room. Looking around the lavishly furnished room he saw the old woman seated with her family, and Steve. As he entered, the chatting stopped as they each stared at him.

'Jesus, you look better. Now come on, hurry up, we're all waiting to eat,' Steve told him.

Darren took his seat at the far end of the antique dining table and listened to the conversation going on around him. 'Where the fuck am I?' he asked in confusion. 'I thought you said you were taking me to Spain?'

'You are in Spain,' Steve confirmed.

'Well, if I'm in Spain, how come I can't understand a single word anyone says then? I speak Spanish well enough, and that ain't like any fucking Spanish I've ever heard.'

Steve translated for the whole table and they all broke out in fits of laughter.

'What's so fucking funny now?' he demanded.

'You are in Spain mate, and you're in true bandit country too, but this is bandit country Spanish style. Welcome to the Basque region.'

Steve translated again for the rest of the company and the old woman stood to introduce her family, but this time in Español, and Darren understood practically every word she said.

'I am Rosa, and I am the head of the family here. These are my sons, José,

Roberto and little Valentino. We are all very pleased to finally meet you Mr. Butch,' quickly adding with a gummy grin, 'now that you finally smell like a man instead of a pig.'

'Ah, the Basque country. Now I get it. I'm in Bilbao then?' he reasoned.

'No, no, you are at my farm. It's close to Santoña, but not that far from Bilbao. I have ordered my boys not to speak Euskara, the Basque language, to you. They will speak only in Español from now on, then we all understand, OK?' Rosa replied.

Darren understood the words, but he was confused by his situation and looked around the table with a "please help" expression on his face.

Rosa explained to him. 'You are here because of the problems you have in Ireland. Did your masters tell you nothing about us?'

Shaking his head, Darren replied, 'No. I know about my problems, but I've no idea why I'm actually here with you. No one told me anything about the Basques at all.'

Steve was watching, obviously deep in thought, as he said, 'Look - I think I'd better explain things. You are here to train their people. The Basques need you to teach your own particular brand of combat to them. But you're also here to keep out of the Brits' way too.'

Rosa went a little further. 'We needed someone with specific skills to train our new fighting men quickly and, when your problem arose in Belfast, we asked for you to come here to us.'

'Yes, but who exactly are "you"? I still haven't got a clue.'

'Oh, I thought you would have guessed by now. We are members of E.T.A. and this is one of our training camps,' Rosa patiently explained to him. 'Have some food now and a good night's sleep. Tomorrow you'll meet the rest of the boys. I have told them all about you, and they are looking forward to the meeting.'

Darren tucked into his meal then sat quietly thinking the last few days over with a good cognac and, of course, a cigarette or two. Shortly afterwards he was shown to his room by the eldest son, José. His bedroom was every bit as palatial as the bathroom and he couldn't believe the high standard of luxury he saw in the old farmhouse. From the outside it looked to be falling down, but everywhere he looked inside he saw valuable antique furnishings. The place really was fit for a king. Sighing as he climbed into the old four-poster bed, he snuggled down and closed his eyes. In an instant he'd drifted off into a very deep and restful sleep.

Early the next morning he was awoken by a gentle knock on his door and he rubbed his eyes his to clear his vision as Valentino entered with a breakfast tray.

'Good morning Mr. Butch. Please take this breakfast and hurry down. You have much work to do today,' he told Darren with a smile.

After eating his fill, Darren sat on the side of the bed, lit a cigarette and drank two small cups of the very strong, dark coffee. He would have preferred tea, but that didn't seem to be an option here. Finished with breakfast, he quickly showered, dressed and started downstairs. He entered the dining room and found the whole family once again waiting for him. He was greeted with handshakes, smiles and good mornings by all, and he even got a kiss on the cheek from Rosa herself. Several coffees and half a pack of cigarettes later, Steve arrived. It was now almost seven thirty, so they left the house and everyone climbed into an old Transit van.

Roberto started the engine and they drove off, making their way up a barren looking cart track. As the van crested the hill, Darren could clearly see four large wooden buildings standing in a neat row in the middle of a lush and green plateau.

The van drew up to the front of the first building and parked. Once they had all climbed out Rosa placed two fingers in her mouth and blew a short, shrill whistle. Moments later men started spilling from each hut. Most of them were still dressing, tucking shirts into trousers and fastening buttons as they went. There were around thirty of them and they appeared to be a tough looking bunch indeed. Quickly they formed a neat row and stood to attention.

Rosa waited a moment and then shouted for everyone to hear. 'This,' pointing at Darren, 'is your new close combat training officer. You will speak only in Español to him. His name is Mr. Butch, he is to be obeyed instantly, and questioned never.' As she stood looking at the "boys," she asked if anyone had any questions.

An incredibly large and tough looking man took one slow pace forward and, staring directly at Rosa, said a string of words Darren didn't catch. Steve whispered a rough translation. 'That man says you are too small and weak to teach him anything about fighting. He says you look like a child, a weakling, you should be sent back to wherever you came from, as he would be much better suited as trainer.'

'Ah, a challenge,' Rosa further explained to Darren. 'He wants to take your job. Do you accept Mr. Butch?'

It seemed to Darren that Rosa wasn't too happy at this turn of events, as though it had challenged her authority, and he was none too pleased himself. He'd had one good night's sleep but still felt weakened after his ordeal in the oil drums. Still, he knew better than to let any doubt show. 'It's all right by me, I don't mind at all,' he yawned in disinterested fashion.

'Yes, but a challenge for power here among our brave E.T.A. freedom fighters means to fight to the death, and the challenger has the choice of weapons. Do you understand this Mr. Butch, and do you still accept?' she asked, checking with Steve to make sure the Irishman fully understood exactly what this challenge meant.

Darren held a hand up to Steve, 'I've got it mate,' he assured him while his mind quickly rationalised the situation. Every fight he'd ever entered was potentially to the death, so nothing new there. Also, if he needed to stamp his authority on the situation, as he clearly did, then he would have chosen the biggest, toughest looking man to make his point anyway. All or nothing, he decided. 'Yer man over there looks like he wants it badly enough, so yes, I've no objections to taking him on at all,' he told Rosa indifferently.

'Combat here, now, and Juan asks for knives, so knives it is,' Rosa announced at the top of her voice as the men quickly formed a circle around Darren and his challenger - their champion, Juan.

As the two men stood in the centre, each staring fiercely into the other's eyes, two very large, mean looking knives, which bore a striking resemblance to world war one era bayonets, were thrown in towards the pair. Juan bent and picked up his knife and tested its edge. He gave an evil grin as he stood and waited patiently. Darren looked down at his knife and shook his head, kicking it away into the crowd. The men watched as he pulled *The Killer* from his pocket and flicked open the blade. He glanced across to Rosa, waiting for her approval of his preferred weapon. She nodded towards him and to Juan, who also nodded his acceptance of the knife, and then gave the command for the combat to begin.

The two men started slowly circling each other. Both adopted the classic knife fighter's pose, bent slightly at the waist, hunched over, ever staring they went with outstretched arms. Each man knew that any mistake, no matter how slight, could be fatal. Slowly and deliberately they circled each other until Juan could wait no longer. With the surprising speed and agility of a cat he lunged at Darren, swinging the huge knife as he went. Aiming for the throat, Juan missed, but the blade did connect and dug deep into Darren's face. The sting of pain blinded him for a split second and a huge spray of blood shot outwards, then slowly trickled onto his neck and down the side of his shirt. The men cheered, baying like animals at the sight of first blood. They were in no doubt that their hero was about to be promoted to the job of head trainer.

For such a big guy, Juan's quick and nimble dive had caught Darren off guard. 'Jesus, that man's fast,' he realised. 'Better pick yer game up son, or you'll end up a dead 'un.' Now fully aware of his opponent's capabilities and speed Darren took a single step backwards as Juan sprang at him again. Nonchalantly he sidestepped the big man. Missing his target completely, Juan fell flat on his face and rolled around in the dirt, all the time cursing aloud as he struggled to regain his footing. The crowd cheered. With a look of pure fury on his scowling face Juan dived yet again, swinging his knife in a vicious arc as he went. Missing by a good six inches he landed smack in the middle of the crowd of men.

Darren calmly stood and lifted his knife arm for all to see, making sure everyone was witnessing this. He folded and then retracted the blade. Gasps of shock were heard from the crowd. 'Juan will surely fillet the boy now,' one of them whispered as the huge man emerged again form the group to find Darren facing him with a closed knife in his hand. This only served to heighten Juan's anger, for he took this to be a direct insult, not only to his fighting ability, but even worse, to his very manhood. He could wait no longer. He gave a terrifying and bloodcurdling scream as he ran like a man possessed, swinging the huge knife once more and aiming directly at Darren's chest. In a flash Darren ducked under the hissing blade as Juan passed and, jumping like a panther, he grabbed him around the neck and clung to him in piggyback fashion. Quickly he raised his hand then delivered a crushing blow to the back of Juan's head with the heel of *The Killer.* Juan was instantly stunned as the savage blow matched that of any hammer. Falling first to his knees, then rolling flat on the ground, he promptly passed out.

A cheer went up from the men. As fickle as any crowd could be, it seemed they now had a brand new champion. Darren stood over his defeated adversary and flicked open the blade once more. He bent and sliced open Juan's cheek from lip to ear. Nothing life threatening, just a little payback for the slice to his own cheek and one that would serve as a reminder of who the new boss was around here.

The men were shouting and cheering, screaming for Darren to deliver the deathblow, the coup d'état, and finish poor Juan. This was, after all, a fight to the death. Darren took his time as he looked around, staring into each one of the wicked, expectant, excited faces. Then, very slowly, he shook his head and closed the knife. He abandoned Juan and walked away towards Steve who had been watching every move made with avid interest.

'You know, I think they picked just the right guy for a fighting instructor,' he smiled. 'When I saw the size of that Juan feller, and the size of that fucking great sword he had, I thought for sure you were a dead-un.'

'The size of a man don't mean anyth…'

Darren was cut off in mid sentence by the sharp crack of a single pistol shot. He and Steve swung round together and stared in surprise. The crowd of men stopped jeering and parted silently as Rosa emerged from the throng, pocketing an old revolver as she walked leaving Juan, now dead, in her wake. Looking at the two shocked men she explained. 'I had no alternative but to finish him. Juan was a good man, but he was a famed knife-fighter and you easily beat him in a knife fight. You even did it without drawing blood, so he was totally embarrassed, disgraced *and* dishonoured. And a man with no honour - well, no telling what he would resort to. Or *who* he would talk to. You understand, no?'

It was obvious to Rosa that the Irishmen didn't like what she had done one little bit. But, they both fully understood why she had done it. The two of them grudgingly admitted this to her. She had been right. Juan had been dishonoured and may have sought his revenge by turning informer - or anything really. Yes, she had acted correctly and they told her so.

Darren still had blood running down his face from his wound so Rosa declared that training would commence the next day. The men headed back to the barracks in silence. The family and the two Irishmen climbed into the van. As they drove back down to the farmhouse not a word was spoken.

Early the next morning Darren was in the van again, his cheek stitched roughly, but efficiently, by Rosa. This time only Steve and Roberto accompanied him and, as they crested the hill, they saw every one of the men outside their barracks, standing to attention, waiting for their new instructor. Steve and Roberto remained at the van, happy just to watch, as Darren left and approached the line of his new pupils.

Standing in front of them, he saluted and asked who was in charge. A man stepped forward; he had what appeared to be only one eye, as he wore a piratical black patch over the left one. 'I am Captain Antonio Rodriguez de la Vasco, and I am senior officer here,' he announced as he saluted. Returning the salute Darren told him to group the men into pairs and prepare for the first day's training. Within a matter of seconds they were paired up. 'Hmm, they seem keen enough,' he thought as he smiled at the speed of the pairing. He was impressed. He had never seen himself as a teacher, but he thought back to the calm, efficient instruction he had received from Collins and the authority that the man had possessed. He had that authority now and knew it was his best ally in his new role of instructor.

Rosa had given him a little more information as she was stitching his cheek the previous afternoon. He wasn't sure he'd taken it all in. Rosa didn't have the gentlest touch and the pain hadn't helped him to concentrate in Spanish.

However, from what he could figure out, E.T.A were desperate for new recruits and they needed them trained quickly. A breakaway faction of their organisation was giving up arms and attempting to reintegrate into the political structure. Rosa did not approve of her government, and Darren could understand that. He didn't approve of his government either. So, here he was with yet another set of freedom fighters and this time he was the teacher.

He gave his first order. 'All weapons are to be removed and placed on the floor in front of the first hut. This includes all knives, knuckledusters and anything else that could be considered as dangerous. You will each then be searched by your respective partners.' The men grumbled a little, but not one of them questioned the order, as they walked over to the front of their barracks and sullenly began emptying their pockets of all weapons, dumping them on the ground before returning to form their pairs. As Darren walked among them he ordered the men to search each other. Only two reported finding remaining weapons on their counterparts. One was a cutthroat razor, which the man in question, Pablo, claimed was not actually a weapon, but rather a personal hygiene aid. The other was a small but deadly lock knife and this, he was told, was just a small good luck piece.

'Put them on the floor with the other weapons,' Darren ordered. The two men reluctantly placed the knife and razor with the rest and returned to the line.

'OK men, this is a close combat course, so show me what you can do. On my command, throw your opponent to the floor and hold him down but do not break any bones.' He looked at the eager men then gave the order. 'Now.'

After several minutes, and lots of grunting and groaning, the men had finished, with each of the pairs having a loser and a winner. Darren looked at them and shook his head, tutting. It had been shambolic, but it was a start. He ordered losers to one side, and winners to the other. He now had two lines of men. Showing his disapproval at the length of time taken to simply knock a man down, he offered a display.

'You,' he shouted, pointing to the biggest man present in the winners' line. 'Step out and face me.' The man did as ordered and he stood towering above Darren. 'I weigh around seventy kilos, you must be what? At least a hundred?' he asked him. The big fellow smiled and nodded his head. 'Knock me down and hold me on my back,' he told him. 'Go on man, now.'

The big guy lunged forward. Darren moved fast; so fast that most of the men didn't actually see what had happened. He grabbed an arm and, using his opponent's weight, easily swung him around and off balance. He forced him to the floor, pinned his arms quickly behind him, knelt across his neck and cut off his breathing. 'This,' Darren said calmly, 'is how to put someone down *quietly.* To kill, just press a little harder until the neck breaks.' Then he lifted the stunned man to his feet, patted him on the back and told him to return to the line.

'You will be allowed no weapons whatsoever, *until* you have learned the basic rules of unarmed combat. They are to be taken away from you and locked up. Is that clearly understood?' The men sheepishly nodded their agreement. 'You need first to practice and learn how to fight like *real* soldiers, instead of toy ones.' Insulting them further, Darren added, 'Because if you lot were facing a class of schoolgirls they'd hospitalise the fucking lot of you.'

Silently, the men stood glaring at him. He wasn't popular; that much was obvious, but he had their full attention as he shouted, 'When I think you are ready, and not until, I will allow you to practice your combat techniques with small weapons, knives, bottles, bricks, and the like. Pistols and rifles will follow, but only when I know you're ready for them. Any questions?' Nothing. Not a single word. Disgraced, the men stood in silence. 'Good, now form again in twos. Watch, listen and learn. I'll be passing by everyone.'

For several hours he drilled them, assessing each man's capabilities and strengths. Captain Antonio Rodriguez de la Vasco proved particularly adept and Darren made use of the respect he clearly had with the rest of the men. Maybe it was that eye patch.

As the first day drew to a close Darren thanked the captain for his assistance, offering him his hand. It was warmly accepted. 'Just one thing,' Darren said. 'Antonio Rodriguez de la Vasco is a hell of a mouthful for me, do you have a shorter name I can use?'

'Yes of course Mr. Butch. You can call me Vassi,' he winked. At least Darren assumed he had winked. It was hard to tell with a one eyed man.

The following days continued in the same vein. Advances were made and backwards steps were taken, but gradually the rabble of bandits began to resemble real fighting men. They'd had the balls and the guts from the start, but it had been without focus or control. He was reminded of himself as he had been just a few short years ago, and he thanked Collins daily for the lessons he had learned and could now pass on. Self-reliance, purpose, concentration, he saw these qualities developing in all the men and he was happy with the progress they were making. The stitches that Rosa had given his face had gone after about a week, but the ugly scar left behind served as a reminder to all of his battle and victory that first day. His orders were accepted without question and the daily training sessions settled into a comfortable routine.

8

A Break in the Routine

Darren entered the kitchen to the smell of coffee that was starting to become so familiar. He doubted it would ever replace tea in his affections but he was developing a taste for the strong, invigorating brew that Rosa always had waiting for him. From old hag, this woman sure had turned into a wonderful hostess and he looked forward to their brief, early morning chats alone before he headed out for the day's training. They had improved his Spanish no end and he was nearly fluent now. He even liked the way she said his nickname. Somehow her pronunciation of "Meester Bootch" took the edge of the dark associations the title held for him.

This morning he entered the room to find that Rosa was not alone and the familiar figure of Vassi stood to greet him. 'Mr. Butch, these are Sixtro and Hector,' he was informed, as two strangers walked forward. 'They are trusted one hundred percent. I vouch for both of them.'

'That's good then,' said Darren, shaking hands and wondering exactly what they were trusted for.

Rosa strolled over to the table and opened a large envelope. 'Mr. Butch,' she announced, 'we have been ordered to do a job and, as Juan is no longer with us, we would like you to assist.' She took several documents and street plans from the envelope and placed them on the table. 'Our orders are to acquire additional funding for the cause,' she explained, 'and here is where the money is to come from.'

Darren followed the bony finger as it indicated a building marked on a plan of the small village of Zalla and his eyes widened in disbelief. It was a bank. He sincerely doubted that the intention was to go in and ask politely for a loan, so that left only one conclusion. 'A bank job?' he spluttered.

'Yes, I think that's what you could call it,' Rosa confirmed.

'I'm no bank robber.'

'No, I am aware of that Mr. Butch. But before you came here to us you were not an instructor either, were you?'

'Well, I'm only saying....'

Rosa cut him short. 'You have been chosen for this work Mr. Butch. Do you have a problem with it? It used to be Juan's job, but you removed him remember?'

'Yes, well, no, I mean,' he began. 'Yes, I'll do it all right. It's just that I'm letting you know that I've never done this before, that's all.'

'Do not worry,' Rosa explained. 'Vassi, Sixtro and Hector are well versed in this type of work. The captain asked for you to join and make their four man team complete once more.'

Darren looked across at Vassi. 'Thanks mate - I think,' he grinned.

The men went over the plan together and, with every remark they made, Darren became more and more aware of the fact that this job had been planned for some time.

'Why this bank?' asked Darren.

'Because tomorrow this small, seemingly insignificant, bank will hold the entire monthly payroll for the S.G. Iron Foundry - and that's a very large payroll indeed,' smiled Vassi.

By the middle of the day each man had gone over his roll several times. Sixtro was the driver. It seemed that he had a natural talent for driving quickly, and an unnatural ability to get out of trouble fast. Vassi and Hector were to perform the actual robbery. And Darren? Well, he was what they quaintly referred to as "crowd control".

'Try to avoid any shooting as the bank will have few clients at the hour we hit, so this should go down very quietly,' Vassi advised Darren. 'However, if anyone should put up a fight, hit them with a... Well, I'm sure I don't need to tell you what to do. After all, that's why I asked for you.'

As the meeting drew to a close Rosa told Darren, 'You can have a good night's sleep tonight Mr. Butch, as you do not have to meet until mid-day tomorrow.' But, in bed that night, Darren had anything but a good sleep. He tossed and turned the entire time. The constant worry of letting down his new crew plagued him. He didn't really want to rob anyone, but the plan had been made and he was included. The following morning he was up at six thirty. He ate breakfast at seven and, in an effort to calm his nerves, drank several cups of strong dark coffee.

Mid-day arrived and Darren walked out into the brilliant sunshine to find Sixtro and Hector waiting for him, happily polishing a late model BMW five series. 'Nice car,' Darren whistled.

'Thank you Mr. Butch. I "borrowed" it from a lady in Santander earlier this morning,' Sixtro grinned.

Vassi arrived. 'Everyone ready?' he asked. The others nodded.

'Here.' Vassi passed each of the men a dark jumper, a black beret and a white facemask.

Hector quickly donned his kit in order to demonstrate it for Darren. The facemask reminded him of the white hoods the Ku Klux Clan wore but, instead of the pointy bit at the top, these were finished off with the black beret. 'Jesus, they look fucking eerie,' Darren shuddered. 'Do I have to?' he asked, looking down at his disguise.

'Of course,' Vassi laughed. 'This is the E.T.A. uniform. We don't want anyone to have any doubts whatsoever who, exactly, robbed this bank.'

'Yes, but I was thinking of wearing a stocking mask ins...'

Vassi cut him off. 'Mr. Butch, if you want to wear ladies underwear that is entirely your business - but not on this job. Wear it in your room. No one here will think any the less of you.'

'I didn't mean to...' Darren stopped short, realising that he was being made fun of. 'OK, OK, you win.'

'Besides,' continued Vassi, 'the very sight of men in white masks and black berets seems to silence any vigilantes very effectively. So much so we rarely have to pull our guns.'

The four men donned their jumpers and climbed into the Beemer, leaving their masks and berets on their knees. Though still nervous Darren didn't have much time to fret, as the drive across to Zalla was a short one. Around forty-five minutes later they were cruising down the main street and heading in the direction of the bank. As they passed, Vassi looked across at the building but the other three kept their eyes fixed dead ahead.

'Good, it's quiet,' he smiled as they went by.

Sixtro drove on for around a mile and then made a u-turn, driving back to park the car a hundred yards or so from the bank on the opposite side of the road. Vassi, Hector and Darren each picked up a tool-bag and set off strolling lazily towards the bank. Though they appeared relaxed each of them was following the instruction to 'keep a sharp look out for anything out of the ordinary.' Darren took "out of the ordinary" to mean hundreds of cops with very large guns. They saw no one. The street was deserted.

As they entered the bank they breathed a sigh of relief. There were only two tellers and five clients standing in line. The men slowly walked to the back of the bank and headed to a long bench covered with old pens, withdrawal slips, deposit slips and scraps of paper. They looked at each other in turn, then nodded and donned the masks and berets.

When they turned, a female teller stared for a second and then fainted. The other teller froze, his face ashen as he stared into the white masked faces of the three bank robbers.

'Dios mio, E.T.A,' a woman screamed at the top of her voice.

'Silence, this is a robbery,' shouted Darren. 'Everyone keep quiet and everybody lives.'

Though he'd never admit it, he was sweating almost as much as the people he was holding up. This was a new and unnerving experience for him.

The silence in the bank was deafening, as everyone kept their mouths shut and their eyes open, each one staring slack jawed at the menacing black machine gun the hooded E.T.A. robber was pointing at them.

Enrique was twenty years old and he was new at the bank. This was only his third week working as a teller and it was definitely his first robbery. He pressed a hidden button below the desk but it seemed to do nothing. He had expected to hear alarms, but there were none.

An older man emerged from a back room and Vassi noted him at once. 'You,' he shouted, 'you're the manager. Open the safe.'

'I, I don't have the k, k, keys,' he stammered.

Vassi walked towards him, slowly waving his pistol back and forth in the man's face and then jamming it firmly into the back of his neck. 'The next thing to come out of your mouth will be either your blood and brains, or the words "here are the keys sir". Now, what's it going to be?' he snarled.

With trembling fingers the man opened a desk drawer. He fished around for a second, then said, 'Here are the keys sir,' as he handed them over.

Vassi snatched them from the man, forcing him to the floor at gunpoint. 'Stay there and keep quiet,' he ordered.

Darren was still standing with his back to the wall, his gun trained on everyone. No one said a word. He watched Hector and Vassi as they quickly disappeared into the rear of the bank. The silence continued and Darren saw the fear in the faces staring at his gun. The female teller came round and a scream threatened to escape her as she stood unsteadily, but her young colleague shushed her.

Around five minutes later Vassi and Hector emerged from the vault, each carrying a large black hold all. 'Stay here at the door, cover them and shoot anyone who moves,' Vassi shouted loudly enough for all to hear. As he passed by Darren he whispered, 'Mr Butch we'll pick you up when we've loaded the car.'

Sixtro had brought the BMW to the front of the bank. 'Everything going OK?' he asked.

'No problem. Quiet as the grave in there brother,' grinned Hector before he and Vassi headed back into the bank and were out again a few minutes later with two more bags which they loaded into the car.

Then the rear light exploded and Vassi jumped violently. 'Shit, cops,' he cursed, as pistol shots echoed around them and a burst of machine gun fire announced the arrival of the Guardia Civil.

'Someone's set off an alarm,' yelled Hector as he and Vassi jumped in the car and Sixtro floored the accelerator, setting off at speed and quickly covering a few hundred yards.

'Stop! Mr. Butch is still in there,' yelled Vassi.

'Too late now,' Sixtro shouted back.

'Stop!' Vassi repeated, and the command in his voice brooked no argument. Sixtro hit the brake and the car slid to a halt.

Vassi was out in an instant, running towards the bank, Butch, and a free flying hail of bullets.

Darren poked his head out into the street at the sound of the first shots, but immediately retreated as the doorframe exploded in a spray of splinters. 'Bollocks, that'll be me fucked then,' he shouted to no one but himself. The noise of gunfire grew for several seconds, but then it began to lessen. He risked another peek outside and couldn't believe what he saw. Neither could the armed police, apparently. There was Vassi running towards them, dodging the bullets that bounced around him and, one by one, they stopped their firing, mesmerised by the bravery they were witnessing.

It took Sixtro a few seconds to comprehend the scene too, but then he rammed the BMW into reverse, screeching to a halt at the door as Vassi was pulling a stunned Darren from the bank. The Guardia Civil regained their senses and the firing started again, just as the two men dived into the car, which shot away leaving burning rubber in its wake.

The back window shattered and gunfire raked the rear of the fleeing car. Hector lurched sharply to one side as he caught a couple of shots.

'You OK?' yelled Sixtro as he drove with all the brilliance that Darren had been promised.

'Nothing a shot of Jim Beam won't fix,' Hector assured him as he sat up again. He was bleeding heavily from his shoulder and the tip of one ear was dangling from a thread of skin.

'Can I have your sunglasses now?'

'Fuck you. They'll still fit me, ear or not. Now just drive you fucking pig farmer.'

Darren knew it would have taken the cops a few seconds to get back in their vehicles and start the chase, giving them a head start, but the speed and control with which Sixtro drove were amazing. Still, they were not out of harm's way yet. 'We have to get this car off the road,' he said, as he noted Hector's blood dripping from the headlining.

'I know, but where? We don't have friends here,' Vassi told him.

'I have family close by,' grinned Sixtro. 'My sister, and she lives just off this road.'

He turned a sharp left and headed down a dusty cart track, coming to a halt a few moments later outside an old farmhouse. He jumped out calling, 'Chucha, Chucha, are you home?'

Jesús María, known affectionately to her family as Chucha, came running from the front door towards the BMW. 'Holy mother of God, what happened my brother?' she asked.

'No time for that, Chucha. We need help,' Sixtro told her.

'Yes, yes of course come in. Hector, can you walk?' she asked in concern as she noticed the injured man in the car.

'Of course I can walk. It's only a nick - or two,' he smiled at the woman.

Once inside the farmhouse Chucha quickly went to work. Her sons had provided her with all the medical skills she needed. Bringing up three rowdy boys in rural Spain required a special knowledge of doctoring, as the closest hospital was miles away. She was used to stitching the cuts and treating the bruises they got fighting and playing. She was also a dab hand at setting broken bones, but thankfully that skill would not be needed today. However, as she cut off Hector's shirt, she quietly gasped. This was bad. Around two inches of horizontal muscle was missing from his shoulder.

'You really need a hospital Hector,' she told him, 'but I'm guessing you can not go to one - no?'

'That's right. Can you just stitch it for me?'

'I can, but it will leave a really ugly scar.'

Hector grinned. 'You think another scar is going to bother me? How about the ear, though? Do you think it is still possible for me to wear my sunglasses?'

'Yes, I think so.'

'Then I need to tell your brother to fuck off again. Is that OK with you?'

'Perfectly,' she assured him.

Around half an hour later she had finished her ministrations and there had been no sounds of sirens screaming down the dirt track, so Sixtro's amazing driving had done the trick. 'Is Pepe at work today?' he asked his sister. 'We need to lose this car.'

'Yes, you go and I'll call him. He'll be expecting you.' She smiled as she kissed her brother goodbye and the four men set out again in the bullet ridden BMW.

A five-minute drive down the dirty, bumpy road took them past a high, corrugated steel fence until they arrived at large steel gates guarded by two snarling, snapping German Shepherds. A handmade sign with letters two feet high proclaimed:

Pepe el Monstruo
Autos Chatarra Quería
Comprado por Dinero en Metalico

Piezas de Automóviles

Basically a scrap metal dealer, Darren reasoned. 'Who's Pepe?' he asked.

'Chucha's husband, my brother-in-law,' Sixtro informed him. 'He cuts up cars, sells parts, deals in scrap and is basically a very handy guy to know. This is him now,' he added, as a large, grease covered man with a full beard opened the gates and waved them through. They parked where he indicated and took the bags of money with them as they left the car.

Pepe embraced Sixtro, kissing him on both cheeks. Then he grasped Hector warmly by his good shoulder. 'Chucha said you might look a little strange today, my brother,' he observed.

Darren watched the greetings and smiled. He was becoming used to the affection men could show to each other in this country, and he liked it. Pepe had called Hector his brother and that might mean they were blood relations, but it could just as easily mean they were two good friends who respected each other. Relationships here were important and it meant a lot to be treated as family.

Sixtro introduced Pepe to Vassi and Butch and then they got down to business. 'Domingo,' Pepe shouted to a slim young man across the yard. 'This BMW, take it for SG,' and only minutes later the once pristine car was crushed beyond recognition, ending up as a cube of metal that was swiftly loaded by forklift onto a waiting truck with "S.G. Foundry" painted on the side.

Darren suddenly laughed. 'Hey, isn't that the company who...' He paused, looking across at Pepe, unsure of how much he could say in front of this man.

"Who kindly helped to fund our cause today,' Hector confirmed as he also noticed the lettering.

Pepe's brows rose in surprise. 'Really?' he questioned as he put two and two together. 'How appropriate. Well, at least you are giving them something for their money, no? Even if it is just a block of scrap metal.'

The men looked at him for a moment, then all broke out laughing. Darren probably laughed the loudest. For the others, Pepe included, an adventure like the one today was obviously nothing new, but to Darren it had been quite an experience. Of course, he'd seen his fair share of action in many ways, but nothing quite like this. Also, he usually worked alone. Teamwork had never really been his thing and, apart from Thomas, he couldn't think of anyone he would truly call a friend. The camaraderie he was witnessing here appealed to him.

Vassi pulled a wad of cash from one of the bags and gave it to Pepe. 'Thank you,' he said. 'Be sure to buy Chucha something nice will you?' Pepe assured him he would and then provided them with a car for their journey home.

Sixtro drove more sedately now and Hector fell asleep in the passenger seat, the pain medicine Chucha had provided making him drowsy. Darren turned to Vassi in the back. 'That was really incredible, what you did today,' he said. 'I've never seen anything like it in my life. It was one Hell of a risk. Why did you come back for me?'

'Because you are my brother,' Vassi informed him simply.

'Thanks man.' Darren was incredibly moved by the sentiment. He didn't think any of his compatriots back home would have done that for him. Not even Thomas.

9

The Message

Back at the training camp the regular routine had resumed and over the following weeks Darren saw continued improvement in the men. They were well into a session of small arms training one day when the sound of an approaching vehicle brought the lesson to an abrupt halt as Valentino arrived in a cloud of dust, jumped from his car and ran to Darren's side. He saluted him and announced, 'Mr. Butch, a message has arrived for you from Ireland. We think it is important. Please return to the house with me.'

'Er, okay,' Darren agreed, somewhat surprised that he would receive a message here. He'd lost track of how long he'd been with Rosa and her men – a month? Two? Certainly long enough for him to believe he was "out of sight, out of mind". OK, so Willy has assured him he wasn't being punished, but the whole degrading oil drum ride and the unceremonious dumping in the middle of nowhere with no warning of what to expect, felt as if he'd been sidelined. Now he had a message? He left Vassi in charge, jumped in the car with Valentino and off they headed back to the farmhouse.

Rosa stood on the porch waiting for Darren and her boys with a pot of hot coffee. 'Mr. Butch,' she began hurriedly, 'I have a radio message for you. I copied it down exactly and I hope you can make sense of it.'

Darren took the note from her bony hand and read it quickly. "13X99KLC. D.M.B.O.B. 786. B.A.P. Cat. T.M. 2091. 29." He looked up at the old lady. 'I'll be needing the use of a car,' he explained, 'I have to take a trip - and have to leave as soon as possible.' He thought he noticed a flicker of sadness cross the wizened face and, surprised that he felt the same, assured her, 'I'll be back as soon as I can.'

'We have two cars that are road worthy,' Rosa offered. 'This one belongs to Valentino,' she indicated an old

Citroen, 'and that little Honda Civic is mine. Make use of either one.'

The battered Citroen looked as though it would be lucky to make it to the training camp, so the Honda was the only choice. 'Is the Civic fully legal?' he asked. 'I don't want to get pulled over by the police because of something stupid like faulty brake lights.'

'With the exception of a broken heater, that Honda is in perfect shape,' Rosa assured him.

'Good, I'll take that one, and a road map if you have one - I need to leave at first light,' he informed the old lady.

Message in hand Darren strolled over to the little Honda. Once alone he slowly re-read his instructions, decoded them fully and consulted the map he found in the glove box. 13X99KLC was the authentication code direct from the boss in Belfast. The rest informed him that he had to meet a known contact at Barcelona airport the following evening.

'Shit - Barcelona. That's over two hundred and fifty miles from here. I hope that Honda makes it,' he mumbled whilst lighting a cigarette. He used the same match to burn the message then he tossed the ashes, grinding them into the dirt with his boot.

10

Catalunya: The Road Trip

Darren was up at dawn the following morning but Rosa was already in the kitchen to supply a hearty breakfast. He exaggerated a yawn to cover the tears he felt coming to his eyes as he was reminded of his mother. He hadn't time for such sentimentality today. He ate quickly and then went to check out the car. The road map occupied the passenger seat, *the Killer,* his pocket, and the .45 automatic pistol sat under the map. He was ready to leave. Rosa gave him a few basic directions, a packed lunch that would feed a family of four, a flask of coffee, then waved him on his way.

As he left the farm-track and pulled onto the main road he shivered. The early morning chill in northern Spain was vicious. Glancing down at the heater he tried each of its three settings, patiently waiting for a much-needed blast of hot air that never came. 'Shit. Cold, very cold and fucking freezing,' he grumbled. Still, everything else was working fine. 'The sun'll be up soon. I won't need a heater then,' he comforted himself.

He pulled onto the main road and overtook a farmer who was repairing his old tractor. Shivering in the cold plastic seat he wiped the condensation from the windscreen. His eyes fixed straight ahead, he paid no attention to the farmer who, as Darren passed, reached down for the handset of his military radio.

The drive was long and uncomfortable, taking around ten hours. Darren was used to the winding roads of Ireland but the Spanish system seemed even worse and the little Honda, valiant though it was, struggled with the never-ending bends and ever-changing gradient. Thankfully, from the outskirts of Barcelona, the airport was well signed and he finally drew into the rough, pot-holed, parking area. He rushed into the terminal building to check on the arrival of Dublin flights. His coded message had been brief, meaning he'd have to figure out some of the details for himself, but the information board greeted him with the good news that there was only one Dublin flight due that evening. Great, that was helpful. The not so helpful news was that it had been cancelled. Fuck. Now what?

The airport already seemed to be closing for the night and he was unable to find any information for the following day, so he just had to assume that his contact would arrive on the next available flight. Should he try to find a hotel or stay where he was? Much as he hated the idea, a night spent in the car seemed to be the sensible option so that he was already in position for the following day. He walked stiffly back to the Honda and silently thanked Rosa for her forethought when she had over-provisioned him for the journey. The coffee was gone, but he still had food. What he needed most, though, was sleep. The long drive had taken its toll. He pulled up his collar and reclined the driver's seat, settling down for the night.

He slept sporadically in bursts of half an hour or so and felt anything but rested when the airport came to life the following morning. He climbed out of the car and stood yawning and stretching before collecting his overnight bag and heading towards the terminal and the men's toilet. A long wash in ice-cold water brought him round and he went in search of flight information. Finding that the next arrival from Ireland would be in four hours he still had time to kill. It was a beautiful morning and the sun here had more strength than he had become used to. A grassy area in front of the terminal looked a welcoming place to rest and ease out his aching limbs, and it seemed he wasn't the only one with that idea as he joined six others already stretched out in various stages of relaxation. Using his overnight bag for a pillow Darren lay back and yawned. In just a few hours he'd have to be alert, but for now he could afford a little more sleep.

Alpha-Six-One watched the Irishman approaching, recognising his target through slitted eyes. 'McCann for sure.' Rolling into the foetal position, he feigned sleep and gave a long, low snore. A few minutes later his target was snoring too. Alpha-Six-One stood, stretched and yawned then, after wiping the freshly mown grass from his jeans, he walked lazily to the terminal. Halting at the door he glanced behind and, seeing no movement from his target, dived into the passenger seat of the old Ford waiting for him. 'It's McCann all right,' he told his partner. Their orders were simply to watch, wait and report.

Awake again following a more restful sleep, Darren strolled back towards the car park. After fishing around in his pocket for a moment he found the ignition key and started the little Honda, taking it to the small waiting area for arrivals. Around thirty minutes later a familiar figure slowly emerged from the building. 'Thomas, you bog Irish git, what the fuck have you got there?' he laughed to himself at the sight of his friend, red-faced and sweating, with one small bag hanging from his shoulder and a huge suitcase trailing behind. He pulled the car alongside him, wound down the window and offered, 'Taxi?'

Thomas faced him with one of his famous "looks". 'Just give me a hand with this fucker instead of acting the cunt will yer Butch,' he snapped.

'Jesus, what you got in the bag, a fucking piano?' asked Darren, as he struggled to get it into the back seat.

Thomas said nothing; instead he climbed into the passenger's side and tutted irritably. Darren thought it best to allow him to regain his breath as he headed the car to the exit.

Eventually, the flush fading from his face, Thomas looked at his friend's suntanned features. 'Fuck me, you've gone native. You look just like a Fuzzy Wuzzy. All you need is one of those fez hats they all wear over here.'

'Spaniards don't wear fezzes Thomas - that's the Morroc... Oh fuck it, man, what's in the fucking bag?'

'My gear, but mostly cash,' Thomas informed him. 'Head for a town called Sitges; it's just south of us.'

'What's in Sitges?' asked Darren. 'Why are we going there?'

'Want the long story - or the short one?' sighed a disgruntled Thomas who obviously was not very keen on the Spanish heat.

'Short one'll do.'

'To kill somcone.'

'Ah.'

Driving along Darren lit a cigarette and waited. Silence. He finished the cigarette, stubbed it out and waited some more. Still silence. Eventually he could take it no longer. 'OK then, fuck it - give me the long story.'

Thomas wound down his window and fanned his face with his hat. 'Did you hear about that bloke from Madrid who took one of our bags a few months back?' Darren shook his head. 'Well, *the boys* sent a bag over here to pay for a couple of containers of fags. This feller was to take the bag and change it up. But instead he fucked off, scarpered with the lot.' Thomas tutted and spat out of the window before continuing. 'Not hide nor hair's been seen of this fucker ever since - until last week that is. Belfast got a report that he's been seen drinking in a bar down in Sitges.'

'And the big ba...'

Thomas cut his friend off. 'The bag I've brought is a cash bag for another container of fags.'

The not so very much longer long story now finished, they drove on in silence, Darren lighting another cigarette as they headed south - carefully following the Sitges road signs. A few hundred yards back the two soldiers followed.

Darren was admiring the sea view as they entered the small, seaside town of Sitges when Thomas called out to him, 'There, pull into that parking spot Butch.' Doing as he was told, Darren slowed then reversed the Honda into one of the available spaces. As he applied the handbrake he noticed they were facing a small, sea front hotel with the name "Hotel Solana" in neon above the door.

'There's where we're off, Butch. Got to meet a bloke called Lupo,' said Thomas as he jumped out of the car, quickly grabbing the two small overnight bags. 'You bring the big un,' he laughed, as he made his way towards the hotel. Two soldiers watched patiently from their car.

Struggling with the weight of the cash bag, Darren eventually caught up with his friend and they entered the hotel together. A bored-looking desk clerk glanced up from his newspaper. 'Si?' he asked lazily.

'Tengo una cita con Lupo' (I have an appointment with Lupo) Darren answered.

'Nombre?' questioned the clerk.

'Butch.'

Thomas was impressed with his mate's apparent fluency in another language. 'See, told you you've gone Fuzzy. You do need one of them fez things.'

'Ah, yes sir, I'll tell Lupo you have arrived, please take a seat,' said the clerk, smoothly switching to English. Once again Thomas took the small bags, leaving Darren to lug the heavy one, as they crossed the lobby to take their seats and wait.

It wasn't long before Lupo arrived, clicking his fingers at the clerk and pointing to the suitcase. The man leaned and whispered something in Lupo's ear, then took the cash bag and disappeared with it. 'The money will be convert to Peseta, you have in two day time,' Lupo explained in halting English. 'The Honda Civic in front, yours no?'

'Aye, it is that,' replied Darren.

'To use car such as this, in Sitges, for work is bad,' Lupo told the Irishmen. 'Need good car with local registration, something that, er, how you say, blends in - no? I have different car, good for you.' With that he walked towards the rear of the hotel beckoning them to follow. Outside in the staff park Lupo pointed to a sleek new Rover saloon. 'This my car. I use every day here in town. It good car for you work,' he explained before giving them directions to "Bar Pascal", the waterfront restaurant their target had been seen frequenting for the last few days. A handshake, followed by a short wave goodbye, and Lupo returned inside his hotel. The Rover left from the rear of the Solana as two soldiers kept watch over the stationary Honda at the front.

On the short drive to Bar Pascal, Darren asked Thomas if he knew the man they were looking for. 'Never laid eyes on him, but I have his name, Ernesto Manuel Ruiz, his description, and a photo.'

They found the bar easily and pulled into a car park on the front, which gave them a good view of the entrance from the road. A few palm trees slightly obscured their line of sight to the terrace, which stood out into the sea, but overall this was a good vantage point. Darren silently blessed Lupo for providing them with a decent car. That old Honda would have stuck out like a sore thumb here as the whole place exuded wealth and a certain cultural feeling or, as Thomas succinctly put it, 'Bit arty-farty here, ain't it?' Expensive cars came and went, people sat under the umbrellas drinking cold beers and eating tapas, and this seemed like a very popular bar. 'Must be the sea view, because it doesn't look cheap,' thought Darren as he lit another cigarette.

11

The Thief

Ernesto rolled over in bed. He loved the feel of silk sheets - sheer heaven. Smirking to himself, the wealthy man sighed contentedly as he cast a lazy gaze at his new girlfriend of the last couple of weeks, the beautiful young senorita dressing in front of him. As she pulled on her panties she stopped for a moment and, with a quizzical expression, she looked over at him and pouted.

'Oh, I'm sorry my darling, here you are,' he told her in his low, Andalucían accented voice whilst pulling a thick wad of cash from his bedside table. 'Same time tomorrow my little angel?' he smiled.

Though the girl smiled seductively back at him, inwardly she cringed and cursed, *'Puto gordo viejo.'* 'Yes, of course my sweetheart,' she answered in a soft, lilting tone. 'Same time. Can't wait.' She leaned over and gently took the money from his hand, then turned and slowly left the bedroom, wiggling her hips as she made her way out of the house.

Safely through the gates, and out of sight of the eyes that had watched her from the bedroom window, she hawked deeply and spat. *'Coño,'* she cursed again, still feeling sick at the thought of the stinking man who'd been pawing at her all night. 'Fat, smelly, filthy, ugly old man,' she hissed as she shivered involuntarily. Still, the money was good. In truth she considered herself lucky, as she hadn't been short of cash since meeting him. All she had to do was look good, smell good and, every once in a while, let him do the depraved and disgusting things he loved to do to her. It was for the money, and only for the money, and she had wondered more than once where it came from. He didn't seem to do anything to earn it. 'It's always cash and he seems to have loads of it,' she considered. 'The next time the filthy pig is snoring, I'll search and I'll find it. I'll take the lot. I'll leave the old bastard broke.' The smile on her pretty face was now genuine.

Alone again Ernesto basked and posed in the midday sunlight, sucking in his belly as he admired himself in his full-length mirror. 'You really are a handsome devil, I can see why the girls go mad for you,' he tittered as he quickly pushed several long strands of hair back over his head to cover his bald patch. 'There, that's better.' He picked up his silk dressing gown and then paused for a second to sniff each armpit. He dropped the garment. Maybe today he'd better take a shower.

The task, quickly completed, he briskly towelled himself dry, slid on his dressing gown and strolled out onto the ornate patio. From his terrace he was able to look down on most areas, the good parts, of his favourite city in the whole of Spain- Barcelona. Slowly he walked up and down the terrace, happily gazing out at the tremendous views. 'Fucking Irish,' he muttered, wondering why on earth he should suddenly think about them on a day like this. 'Coffee time - and a smoke,' he announced to no one but himself.

He made his coffee very carefully. The beans were ground meticulously and exact amounts had to be used. When it came to coffee, he was the best. He was a perfectionist. Sitting with a look of pure ecstasy on his face he grinned to himself as he savoured the rich taste. He knew beyond doubt that no one made coffee like he did. 'And now for that smoke,' he decided, as he made his way to his newly purchased, antique humidor. Selecting a big, fat Cohiba he gently rolled the cigar between his fingers, holding it first to his ear, 'sounds good,' then to his nose, as he inhaled the rich tobacco scent, nodded his approval and smiled. 'Yes, a Cohiba would be nice today.' He strolled out once more onto his terrace and gave another long, loving gaze across the city and sighed. 'Ah, life really is good,' he laughed, puffing happily away.

He sat in the shade of an umbrella, contentedly smoking the huge cigar and feeling more relaxed by the minute. His thoughts dwelled on the perfect body of the girl who had just left, though her name escaped him for the moment. She was one of many who had graced his bed over the last few months and he was enjoying the variety. It was so much better than the monotony of having a wife, he decided, and was a little confused by the sense of melancholy, tinged with dread, that suddenly descended to ruin his mood. Drowsiness overtook him and, yet again, those fucking Irish popped into his mind, as did that awful day several months ago.

***

The Awful Day

Having woken very late, he found he was alone in bed. 'Darling, where are you?' he shouted softly. There was no reply. She wasn't in the bedroom. Frantically he searched the entire house and he began to panic - until he found the note. 'Goodbye Ernesto, I've gone. Anna.' That was it. No explanation, no apology, no words of comfort, no suggestion of sorrow. She was simply gone.

At first he just didn't believe it, but after days of trying everything to locate her, ringing anyone he could think of, acceptance finally sank in. What he couldn't figure out, though, was why. There was no rational reason for her to go, to leave him alone like this. He knew he'd been a good husband. He'd never involved her in his business dealings – good Lord, she didn't even know what he did for a living anyway. He'd let her be happy in her kitchen, just as she wanted. That clearly ruled out another man, so why had she gone?

Over the next few weeks he went to pieces, drinking continually and never leaving the house. Constantly he contemplated the "why" and only one reason made any sense. Money. Things had been a little tight for the last few months. That new car Anna had needed had cost him a fair bit. Then there had been the new clothes so that she was nicely turned out when she went to those ladies' charity dinners that had been taking up more and more of her time. He'd been thinking of asking those Irish bastards for a bigger commission for a while. At first the money had seemed good for a couple of days of his time, but now he had extra expenses and they needed to know that. He'd never let them down and it was about time they appreciated his loyalty a bit more. If they'd only paid him what was fair, his Anna would never have left. This thought played over and over in his mind as he sat in the silent, empty house. He hadn't seen a soul for weeks and no one had even bothered to call him back after his frantic efforts to locate his wife. The phone hadn't even rung once – and then it did.

He sprinted like an Olympian to catch the call, knowing it had to be her. She was coming home.

'Anna, Anna, where are you? Please come back to me - I love you,' he cried into the receiver.

'Ernesto? Ernesto? - Hello? What the fuck are you on about? Stop your ranting man, I can't understand a fucking word you're saying,' came the Irish voice on the other end of the phone.

Taking a deep breath Ernesto paused, swallowed, and then composed himself. 'Hello, who is this speaking?' he enquired in English now.

'Ah, that's better. It's me - Chucky from Belfast. What the fuck were you gabbling on about?'

'Oh, nothing, I wasn't shouting at you - the gardener knocked over my new ornament, that's all,' he lied.

'Oh, so everything's still all right over at your end then?'

'Yes, of course it is, what do you need?' he asked Chucky in as happy a voice as he could manage.

'Same thing as always, mate, but this time we've got two instead of one. Can you handle that?'

For the last four years, Ernesto's job had been to exchange the Irish organisation's cash into local currency, and with that they bought cigarettes by the container. They never had a single problem with him - he was trusted completely. Chucky and the other bosses considered him to be "as good as gold". Two containers translated to ninety six thousand cartons, Ernesto quickly calculated, and that meant an awful lot of cash, the very subject that had occupied his thoughts for these last, lonely weeks.

He paused only a second. 'Yes, of course I can handle it,' he told his contact, but that will be a large package. The transfer will take longer than normal.'

'That's okay,' Chucky assured him. 'We'd expected that. How long do you think?'

'Well it's usually two days, so I think this would be four or five,' he suggested, assessing how he could use that time to carry out the plan that was forming in his mind.

'No problem,' Chucky agreed. 'Can you be ready Thursday, same time, same place, same contact?'

'Yes.'

'That's great. I'll talk to my boss about a bigger percentage this time to cover the extra days,' Chucky offered cheerfully.

'Too little and far too bloody late,' would have been the honest reply. Instead Ernesto said, 'That's good of you,' hoping he had the right amount of gratitude in his voice.

'Okay, call me when it's done and I'll sort the order,' Chucky concluded, and the call was over.

As he replaced the receiver, Ernesto smiled for the first time in weeks. It was fate. It had to be. A double load, just when he'd decided that money was the answer to his problems. And that condescending little shit, offering him a bigger commission now, after all this time. He should have been on a proper cut from the beginning. He took all the risks, didn't he, showing his face around to change their filthy money. He'd never let them down and he knew they trusted him one hundred percent. Ha, stupid Irish cunts. He'd show them.

The simple plan came together quickly in his head. He would arrive at Reus airport and collect the money from one of the Irish - as he always did. His old Land Rover would be crammed full of cash and he'd drive off alone to visit La Jonquera, the little town between France and Spain that was littered with various small banks and bureaus in which he changed the currency from Northern Ireland sterling into pesetas. He would still do that. Irish sterling wouldn't be any good to him, so he still needed to make the exchange, but now came the clever part. For years those dumb, Irish bastards had thought it took two days to change the money, but it only took one. The second day had been spent at a whorehouse along the coast where he treated himself from the little extra he took on the exchange rate. Just one peseta per note; he'd never been greedy. This time, with double the cash, he probably would need two days, but he wouldn't need five and that gave him all the time he needed to get away.

They knew that he lived in Madrid, and he would be going anywhere but. His house was rented and he didn't care about it. Since Anna had left it was no longer a home anyway. None of those bog stupid Irish could speak any Spanish. That's why they needed him. What was it with English speakers who just assumed everyone would communicate in their language? All he needed to do was disappear forever into the depths of central Spain, or maybe even Portugal, and they'd never find him. He'd have more money than he'd ever dreamed of, and with money he could keep a woman happy. He'd never be lonely again.

***

The cigar was finished and Ernesto glanced at his Cartier watch, wondering where the time went. Reliving his plan to con the Irish, which had played out to perfection, had lightened his mood and the feelings of melancholia had passed. Now he was hungry and thirsty. 'First food - then a beer or two - or maybe even three,' he said, laughing at his own joke. He changed from his robe into his day clothes and began a leisurely stroll through his manicured garden then down the stone steps and into his garage, where he paused to admire his shiny

Mercedes. He couldn't help it. All these long years he'd wanted one, he'd drooled over them - and now, there it sat, gleaming and waiting for no one but him. 'Mɪɪ, I love this car,' he whispered as he opened the door and idly slid behind the wheel. The cool feel of the leather seats through his clothes made him smile. All was perfect. He donned his Ray Bans, admired his reflection in the rear view mirror and reversed out of the garage.

There were several good places to eat and drink close by, but he'd recently found his new favourite spot about an hour away in the exclusive seaside town of Sitges. He'd been five or six times now, and he loved the expensive air of Bar Pascal and the elite clientele it encouraged. He smiled to think how much his life had changed over the last few months. He was now one of the elite and he had women whenever he wanted them. The best thing that ever happened was when that bitch of a wife left him.

12

The Stakeout

The Irishmen had been sitting in the car for about an hour now and Darren was bored. Lazily he lit yet another cigarette then, mid yawn, as he was about to flick the match out of the window, a new golden Mercedes Benz sports car arrived and parked in a spot close to the terrace of Bar Pascal. As the driver emerged, Thomas held up the photo again. 'Finally,' he sighed. 'I think that could be our guy.'

They watched the man walk to the terrace, waving at a well-dressed couple as he went. The couple responded with a half-hearted greeting and then concentrated intently on their meal. The man found a table and sat alone under a parasol directly in their line of sight. Darren looked closely at the photograph in Thomas' hand, then at the man and then back at the photograph. 'Yes, I think it's him,' he agreed, 'but we've got to know for sure. Wait here and don't take your eyes off him.'

He left Thomas in the car and walked casually towards the terrace, stopping just before he reached it to stand behind one of the palms and look back at Thomas in the car. His friend gave him the thumbs up. Good, that meant he couldn't readily be seen by any of the diners. Of course, he couldn't see them either, but Thomas could. 'Oye, Ernesto,' he shouted loudly. Several heads turned in his direction, faces clearly showing confusion or disdain that someone should be so vulgar while they were eating.

Ernesto jumped when he heard his name, glancing round in unison with his fellow diners, then he inhaled sharply and stared quickly back down at the menu. Had he heard correctly? Was that his name? Unlikely, surely. He was known here as Senor Ruiz. His was a common enough name, of course, but still it was a little unsettling. There was no further shout and everyone was eating, drinking and chatting once more as Ernesto pulled the menu closer to his face and looked around again. He could see nothing out of place and finally persuaded himself that he must have been mistaken. The waiter came to take his order and he put the incident to the back of his mind.

Another thumbs up from Thomas gave Darren the all clear to leave the shelter of the tree and make his way back to the car. 'Well?' he asked.

'His name's Ernesto, that's for sure, and he looked nervous as Hell,' Thomas reported.

'That's good enough for me.'

'Me too,' Thomas agreed as the two men settled down to continue their wait.

'Did you hear about our Duggy?' asked Thomas after a long period of silence.

It was rare for his friend to initiate a conversation and Darren asked in surprise, 'No, what's up?

'He's dead - found on Crumlin Road - shot dead.'

'What the f...? When? Why didn't you tell me before, man? 'Duggy dead? What the fuck was a man like him doing on Crumlin Road?' Darren's jaw dropped as he fumbled to ask all the questions that sprang to his mind. He'd known Duggy Mallone almost as long as he'd known Thomas. Good bloke, strong for the cause and certainly not someone who'd stray into that part of Belfast. Running parallel to Shankill Road, Crumlin was fiercely Protestant and highly dangerous for any Catholic.

'Aye, he's dead all right, day after you left, I think. Shot in the head, and nobody has a clue what the fuck he was doing there,' Thomas said, his voice low and monotone

Darren stared at his friend, waiting to see if there was more to come, but the conversation was over. He left Thomas to his thoughts.

The sun had set and Bar Pascal was closing before their target rose, the last to leave. The Irishmen were stiff and hungry after so many hours sitting in the car and they were relieved that their vigil was coming to an end. More than once they'd felt conspicuous, just sitting there like that, and had discussed going into the bar themselves. The idea was discarded, though. Lupo's car blended in nicely with their surroundings, but neither man had been prepared for the unofficial dress code they observed and they would have been totally out of place on the inviting terrace. Also, Thomas' lack of Spanish and thick Irish accent would have been hard to disguise. 'Besides, I don't think we could afford it mate,' Darren had reasoned.

Finally they watched Ernesto approach his car. He seemed a little unsteady on his feet, which was hardly surprising considering the number of drinks they'd witnessed. He dropped his keys twice as he fumbled to open his door and didn't even seem to notice as Darren pulled the Rover up behind him. Thomas moved quickly, exiting the car and clubbing the man from behind.

Ernesto came round to darkness and a throbbing head. He couldn't remember getting home. That was hardly a first, but he must have really laid one on this time as he hadn't even made it to his comfortable bed and had obviously passed out on the floor, which felt like it was moving. God, he hoped he hadn't pranged his beautiful car. He started to stretch, but was confused that he didn't seem able to move. Vomit rose from his stomach to his throat, but he was forced to swallow it again. He couldn't open his mouth. What the Hell was happening to him?

Seconds turned into minutes as he struggled to comprehend the situation. He felt a roughness round his wrists and, forcing his tongue through his lips, detected a stickiness as though his mouth was sealed. But it was the way the floor suddenly lurched, throwing him upwards just an inch or so before his head connected with a ridiculously low ceiling, which finally clarified his position. He was bound and gagged and he was in the boot of a car. What the fuck?

Slowly, through the fog of his mind, a memory formed. Someone had called his name. Someone knew where to find him and knew who he was. His confusion cleared and was quickly replaced by panic and then terror. The scream formed in his throat but all that emerged was a muffled wail. He fought his bonds fruitlessly. Nothing would give as he wriggled and thrashed in his confinement until he felt the car coming to a stop. A few seconds later the boot opened and a weak moonlight illuminated two faces staring down at him. He recognised neither. Strong arms took hold of him and dragged him out into the night and he shook uncontrollably as he was forced into a kneeling position.

As one of the men spoke to him, he found he couldn't understand a word. It was English, he was pretty sure, but he had never heard such a heavy accent. Then the second man spoke, and his words were clear. 'Where's our fucking money?' This time the accent was obvious. He'd had many conversations with similar voices. Whatever the next stage above terror was, Ernesto wasn't sure, but he entered it now. He'd known it while still in the boot, but now there was no doubt. The Irish had found him and it was all over.

As tape was pulled from his mouth, he heard himself screaming incoherently in a mixture of Spanish and English, pleading, praying; saying he was sorry over and over again. He glanced wildly from side to side, seeing nothing but dark fields and a deserted road. There was clearly no escape and his mumbled pleas continued.

'Shut the fuck up,' yelled the man who was easy to understand. 'Where's our fucking money? Dónde está nuestro dinero?'

He was surprised to hear his native tongue and he stared into the cold eyes of the man speaking to him. 'I spent it,' he finally managed.

'All of it?'

'I'll get it back for you. I promise. I'll find it somewhere. I'll repay it. I'll get it all back. I'll….'

Thomas' fist silenced him. 'Fuck you and fuck the money. You were trusted and you stole, but you stole from the wrong people didn't you, you idiot?'

Darren began to translate, but it was clear from the man's terrified eyes that the point had been made. 'Please let me go,' begged Ernesto.

Thomas ignored the plea. He continued in a low growl, Darren now translating every word as sentence was passed. 'Orders from the boys in Ireland. Even if you had the money, you're gone. Even if you could repay every penny, no one steals from the boys and lives. What sort of message would that send, eh?'

Ernesto looked from one man to the next. He couldn't speak now, but the terror in his eyes mingled with resignation and an acceptance of his fate. Tears rolled down his cheeks and a wet patch appeared on his trousers.

'Butch,' said Thomas, the one word conveying the final order.

As he stood in front of the kneeling man, Darren pulled *The Killer* from the pocket of his jeans. He pressed the release switch and its razor-like blade flew out. Though Ernesto's tears continued, he made no further sound as his lips moved in silent prayer. Thomas knelt before him and removed his possessions: rings, wallet, car keys. This needed to look like a robbery for the local police. Anyone who mattered back home would be aware of the execution and that a point had been made. Ernesto closed his eyes and waited as Darren walked behind him, pulling his head backwards and exposing his throat. 'Are you ready?' he whispered.

With a ragged breath, Ernesto uttered his last word on earth. 'Si.'

When the death stroke wasn't delivered the very next second, Ernesto experienced a small moment of hope.

'Butch, what the fuck's wrong with you man?' he heard, and then it was over.

Thomas watched the flashing arc of *The Killer* and jumped to the side to avoid the trajectory of the dark blood spraying like a fountain from the gaping wound. 'Fuck me,' he whispered as he felt the colour drain from his face. Back home he'd witnessed several shootings and God only knew how many beatings, but this was his first throat slashing and he was surprised by how ghastly it was. He stared in fascination as the body twitched in front of him, the neck open almost to the spine. 'Still, the man is a fucking idiot, expecting to get away with robbing the I.R.A. The boys have long memories.'

'Was,' corrected Darren.

'What?' asked Thomas, only then realising that he had spoken his thoughts aloud.

'*Was* a fucking idiot,' Darren clarified.

'Oh, aye - er, right,' Thomas slowly nodded in agreement. Revenge now served, and the latest load of cigarettes paid for earlier, meant one thing. He could go back home and out of this fucking awful heat. He couldn't wait.

The men hid the body in bushes at the side of the road. It would eventually be discovered, but they knew it wouldn't be soon. They were in the middle of nowhere. Their task completed, they drove away in their accustomed silence. Then, for the second time that day, Thomas was the first to speak. 'What the fuck was wrong with you back there, Butch? You hesitated.'

'Nah,' Darren assured him. 'Just wanted to get him into the light for you. Didn't want you to miss the event.'

'Thanks mate.' And the silence resumed.

About half an hour later they sat facing Lupo over the dining table of the Hotel Solana, eating hungrily.

'That was a fucking long day. I'm fucking starving,' Thomas said through a mouthful.

'We should be fucking well better fucking provisioned next fucking time,' Darren suggested.

'Shouldn't be a fucking next time. That bastard's done and it'll send a message to any wanker who thinks he can rip off the fucking boys in future, eh?'

'Stupid cunt,' agreed Darren.

Lupo looked from one to the other. He knew his English wasn't great, but he was beginning to think he didn't understand anything at all. What were those guys talking about? 'Your job here is finished, no?' he ventured, hoping he didn't look as confused as he felt.

'Aye, it's done,' confirmed Thomas as he slid the keys to the Rover across the table. 'Thanks for the car. Hope we haven't left too much of a mess in the boot.'

Lupo smiled. He understood that he was getting his car back, so that had to be a good thing. Then his smile broadened to a grin as Darren, whom he found much easier to understand, passed him a second set of keys.

'Keep it. Consider it a bonus for your help,' he explained.

'Ah yes, Mercedes, it bring good price in Africa. I send tomorrow, thank you very much gentlemen.'

Lupo left them shortly afterwards and they retired to their rooms for the night.

It was an early start again the next day but they emerged well rested and strolled through the car park to the waiting Honda. 'Wish we could have kept the Mercedes,' Darren mused. Still, the trusty little car came to life and the morning here was warm and pleasant, so no need to bemoan the non-existent heater this time. They set off in the direction of Barcelona.

From a hotel on the opposite side of the street, two men watched the Honda drive away before walking to their own car. Keeping well back, Alpha-Six-One and his partner also headed to the airport.

It wasn't long before Darren pulled up at the terminal and prepared to say goodbye to Thomas. 'Flight's due in about two hours,' he said, checking his watch. 'You need me to hang around?'

'You want to come in and hold my fucking hand or something?'

'I'm definitely not holding "or something",' Darren smiled. "So, we're done then. Nothing more to say."

'Well I do have one question. Haven't wanted to stare, mate, but what the fuck happened to your face?' Thomas asked.

Darren fingered the scar on his cheek, replying nonchalantly, 'Oh, this little cut? Nicked it with me razor shaving.'

'Ah,' Thomas grinned back. They said their goodbyes and, a moment later, he was gone.

13

Back on The Road

Darren prepared for the long ride back home and was surprised to realise that he had missed Rosa and the men. His fingers moved to the scar once more as he remembered the dead Spaniard who had given it to him, although now he had a different dead Spaniard on his mind. He'd glossed over the incident with Thomas, but there was no doubt that he had hesitated before cutting Ernesto's throat and he didn't know why. He tried to distract himself with the radio, but every station produced nothing but static. Bollocks. All he had to listen to was the incessant hum of car tyres and the protestations of the little Honda's engine as it again tackled the winding, hilly roads of northern Spain. The effect was hypnotic and he couldn't help but dwell on his life and the strange event yesterday.

'Maybe what you need, Darren me lad, is a change of jobs,' he thought, yet what was it that suddenly made him question his role? He was a killer with a cause and he was good at it. He fought for the boys, and the boys fought for him. Every kill, every victory, was another sweet moment of revenge against the bastards who had taken his mammy's life. And then it hit him. This last killing hadn't served his need for revenge. It had been about money, plain and simple. Sure, that money would have bought guns and those guns would have killed Protestants, but it was starting to feel like a stretch. The dead man had been a thief, no doubt, and a stupid thief at that, but he wasn't British, he wasn't U.V.F, he wasn't R.U.C. and he was pretty damn sure he wasn't Protestant. That looked like some serious Catholic praying he'd been doing just before his death. Basically this man wasn't his enemy and he suddenly felt he'd been – what? Used? Yes, that was it. He felt used.

Darren drove on discontentedly. This was an unsettling realisation and he didn't like it one little bit. Even worse, he didn't know what the fuck he could do about it. Should he really ask for a new job? How about a bit of smuggling? No, that wouldn't meet his need and it wouldn't make him happy again. It was odd to consider that he had been happy until yesterday and, even stranger, to admit to himself that the happiness seemed rooted in a small, Spanish settlement to the north with a wizened old woman and a group of rough, angry men. Could he persuade the bosses that he should be left alone up there to get on with it and that, just maybe, his killing days were over? Mm, it would take some thought. One thing he was sure of, though. Word of his hesitation would soon reach Willy, because he knew his cover story hadn't fooled Thomas in the slightest. He may be a mate, but he was a soldier first.

Alpha-Six-One glanced across at the other soldier. 'Looks like he's heading back home,' he noted as the Honda turned off the main road north from Barcelona. He picked up the radio handset and keyed in the code. 'He's turned north-west,' he reported, providing road information from the map in his lap. 'Yeah, real quiet,' his partner heard him confirm.

'We gonna get the go any time soon?' he asked as Alpha-Six-One finished the transmission.

'Yeah, I reckon. Transport's been waiting, but they need to check position. For now just keep following and keep your fucking distance.'

'That's not going to be so easy now. At least the main road had some traffic. This road's too bleedin' empty.'

'Well that's gonna come in real handy real soon,' Alpha-Six-One smiled.

The tail continued and the driver nearly ground to a halt at one point to avoid catching up to the Honda, which didn't have the power to overtake a slow moving white Ford Transit van that appeared in front of him on a particularly hilly, windy stretch of road. Thankfully it turned off down a farm track and, at that moment, the radio flashed a red call signal. Alpha-Six-One answered, okayed and ended with 'Roger that'. 'At fucking last,' he breathed. 'Follow that Transit.'

The Honda was well ahead and out of sight as the soldiers left the car and headed for a quick debrief. 'He is to be taken alive - is that fully understood?' The commanding officer concluded. The soldiers nodded, collected crash helmets and a Norton Commando motorcycle from the body of the Transit, and headed back out on the road. The van followed.

Darren was so deep in thought that he didn't notice the large black motorcycle until it started to overtake him. The bike's loud, growling exhaust noise quickly shook him back to reality. 'Shit man, get yer fucking head on,' he snapped, reprimanding himself. He glanced in the rear view mirror, but saw only a Transit van way back in the distance. 'Wake up you tosser and keep your fucking eyes open.'

He pulled over a little as the bike passed him and he noticed the pillion passenger's head turn. Then he saw the short, black pipe protruding from his knee. 'Shit, a gun, a fucking gun,' he screamed as he desperately swerved the little Honda across both lanes attempting to get out of the line of fire. But it was too late. A puff of smoke from the gun barrel and his front tyre was blown out. The Honda's steering wheel took on a life of its own as he desperately tried to control it, but he had no chance. The little car zigzagged wildly across the road before catching the ditch, spinning like a top and hitting a tree with its front corner, producing a savage end over end, theatrical roll. Eventually the Honda slid to a stop, lying upside down on its flattened roof.

Alpha-Six-One hit the brakes. Tyres screamed in protest as he turned and gunned the Norton back to the side of the battered Honda. He kicked the side stand down and sat for a moment as he inspected the mangled wreckage. 'Jesus, I'll bet that fucking woke you up,' he grinned.

The Transit arrived on the scene just as Alpha-Six-One was leaning into the wreckage, asking with mock concern, 'Hey, are you OK in there Paddy?' Darren, temporarily blinded with blood from a deep gash on his head, could see nothing. He certainly didn't see the vicious punch as it was delivered, shattering his nose and closing one eye. He blacked out.

'Murdering Paddy bastard,' Alpha-Six-One snapped as he dragged the bleeding Irishman from the car. The men quickly bound and gagged Darren, throwing him roughly into the back of the Transit. Leaving the bike and the wreckage behind them, the van and its occupants left the scene, heading west.

Around five minutes later the driver pulled the Transit off the road and parked in a cloud of dust. The stony clearing chosen for the pick up was devoid of trees and the van's occupants waited until they heard the "whoop, whoop" of a helicopter approaching. It landed and was on the ground for only a few seconds as Darren's limp body was quickly carried and dumped unceremoniously into the chopper. Alpha-Six-One climbed in after him and took a seat directly above the bleeding, bound, gagged and bruised form of the infamous "Butcher of Belfast". Not so fucking hard now, are you - fucking murdering bastard,' he spat.

Darren's eyes flickered momentarily as he began to regain consciousness. Looking down at him Alpha-Six-One tutted. 'No you don't Paddy. Back to sleep, there's a good lad,' he laughed as he delivered a brutal kick to the side of the Butcher's head. Darren was out cold again.

14

The Prison Warden

Eddie McQuillan was a changed man, and it wasn't just his appearance. He'd been lucky, apparently. 'No head trauma. Just one eye gone,' he'd been informed. Lucky? Just? There was no "just" about it as far as he was concerned. In fact there was nothing just in this whole fucking world if that McCann bastard was still out there while he lay helpless in a hospital bed, blinded by the bandages swathing his face. For three days, with only darkness for a friend, he brooded on his loss and the hatred he felt for the man who had robbed him of his eye. Doctors and nurses visited, his dressings were changed and the darkness continued, invading his soul. Hatred turned to thoughts of vengeance and then to determination. He needed to get back to work and track down that murdering son of a bitch. On the day the bandages were removed he faced his reflection, the gaping eye socket unable to stare back at him. He could feel the anxiety of the doctor who had removed the dressing, clearly fearing an emotional collapse, but none came. He smiled as he was given the patch to cover his disfigurement and the doctor pronounced a remarkable recovery.

He walked from the hospital the next day and was soon called to see his superior officer, Commander Cavanaugh.

'How are you holding up, Eddie?'

'I'm doing fine, sir,' he assured him; his voice low and even. 'I think the look kinda suits me.'

'Indeed it does,' his commander agreed with relief. He had expected anger from this big, imposing man and wasn't sure how he would have dealt with it. What he heard was more than acceptance, more than an ability to cope, it was almost like relish and he had to admit that the eye patch only served to enhance the aura of menace. He just hoped the even mood would continue with the news he had to give. 'Your medical report is good, A1, but it's been discussed and, well, a return to active service on the force is out of the question.'

'Sir. No way. I'm ready to go back. I need to go back. You can't retire me,' McQuillan began, his teeth clenching, the anticipated anger starting to show.

The officer stalled him with a raised hand. 'It's not a pension, Eddie. We don't reward bravery like yours with the brush off. We have a new job for you; one where we feel your talents would serve us well. There's an opening at the Maze for a deputy warden and the job's yours if you want it.'

McQuillan's good eye closed slowly, trying to concentrate his mind on the words he was hearing. This was wrong. This wasn't what had kept him going in hospital. 'A prison guard? You want me to be a fucking prison guard? A jumped up nanny to some low-life shits,' he finally managed.

Profanity to a superior officer was frowned on, but Cavanaugh ignored the offence. 'It's a promotion, Eddie, more money. Look at it that way. It could have been worse. I've fought to keep you out from behind a desk. At least this way you'll still be hands on with the punishment.'

McQuillan took a beat. 'Hands on, sir? Literally hands on?'

'What happens in the Maze, stays in the Maze,' Cavanaugh informed him. 'I can say no more than that.

He had been Deputy Warden at the prison for about a month, and he loved it. It wasn't what he had dreamed of in his hospital bed. Oh no, it was much, much better. Many of his colleagues disliked the routine, the daily grind, but Edward "Eddie" McQuillan thrived on the relentless repetition. Each day began with him slowly dressing in his uniform, assessing his appearance in a full-length mirror, adjusting the eye patch to exactly the right angle. He would arrive at the prison immaculately presented, but he'd had to buy several extra uniform shirts. Sometimes the blood just wouldn't come out.

His daily routine had developed and the exactness pleased him. He drove to work carefully, meticulously obeying the speed limit, never wanting to attract attention, always checking his surroundings. Out here he must blend in until he arrived at his domain, his private sanctuary. In there, no one questioned him and he had a growing collection of faces in his head, each one twisted in pain as he did his job of trying to extract information from captured I.R.A terrorists. He smiled to himself. He wasn't actually that good at his job, though it seemed no one dared call him out on it. He couldn't think of one useful piece of information he'd extracted, because he simply wasn't interested in what they had to say. All he wanted was to see those faces, each one of them turning in his mind to the face of the man he hated, the man who had stolen his eye.

He arrived in the prison and parked in his reserved spot. He was special here. He was somebody. Kenny Allen had arrived for his shift a few moments earlier and already had the kettle on as Eddie entered the small office. He liked this kid. He was quiet but tough and he always knew how to turn a blind eye. 'Good morning Kenny,' he offered.

'Oh, it's a good morning indeed sir,' Kenny replied. 'Take a look at the new intake.'

Eddie scanned the list of the roster board. Three names, two of which meant nothing, but the third, oh the third. The Maze prison would today be taking custody of one Darren McCann.

Darren came round in a small, dank room and he had no idea what day it was. The last thing he remembered clearly was seeing that gun pointing at him and then there was a hazy recollection of a loud, incessant whirring noise. His head throbbed and he knew he'd taken several beatings, but the taste in his mouth suggested he'd been drugged as well. He tried to assess his surroundings but, though he could detect light, he could see nothing. There was a tight sensation on his mouth, so he knew he was gagged, while the scratchy feel of rough cloth confirmed that he was blindfolded. He tried to move, but his arms and legs were securely bound to something that was holding him in a seated position. He fought to banish the fear that enveloped him, but he was in the shit. Of that there was no doubt.

***

Darren was still unconscious in the small prison cell as Turner walked slowly from his antique shop, the sedate tread belying his thoughts. He fought the impulse to rush, knowing that he must always remain in character, but he needed to travel north as quickly as possible.

'How the Hell did that happen?' he'd snapped down the phone only moments earlier. 'Deniable operation isn't supposed to mean complete screw up.' He'd heard the intake of breath on the other end of the connection and realised he'd surprised the caller with his tone. Everyone knew that he hated bad language and his, though mild, had been unusual for him. He'd calmed himself quickly. It would do no good to let his anger get the better of him. 'I'm sorry. It will be handled. Make sure that chopper's ready,' he'd concluded.

FInally in the air and heading to Belfast he only hoped he wasn't too late. So much planning had gone into this operation and he couldn't see it fail now. McCann was the prize he'd been after. Years of intelligence gathering and assessing the background of potential recruits had brought Turner two successful 'traitors', one of whom had given him the information that led him to concentrate all his efforts on the young Darren McCann. Everything he knew told him this was the one – not naturally allied with the opposing force, but trained by them into just the kind of ruthless killing machine he needed. He had thick files of names and dates. He knew all about Collins, though he hadn't touched the man. He was handy left in place, doing half the job for him. He assumed Collins would know that one of his earlier apprentices had changed sides. If he was successful with a second protégé, McCann, he had a feeling Collins would disappear without any help from him.

The plan had been good. A mercenary, deniable squad had done their job well, trailing the target until just the right moment and then extracting him. Where it had gone wrong between then and now, Turner didn't know, but somehow McCann wasn't where he was supposed to be. It probably came down to some pen pusher doing his job just a little too efficiently. Instead of being off the radar in the secret headquarters of British Intelligence, Darren McCann, Butcher of Belfast, had entered the system as just one more terrorist and now he was in the Maze.

***

Eddie McQuillan stood quietly in the small room, watching the slight movements that indicated his prey was waking up. Good old Kenny would keep everyone off his back and he had as long in here as he needed. This was going to be quite a day. He waited patiently as the man on the chair started to move more noticeably and then to wriggle frantically against his bonds and it was clear that he was fully conscious. Still Eddie stayed silent. He didn't want to rush this. He had perfected his method and routine over the last month and he was not about to deviate from it now. Indeed the thought of any deviation bothered him. Everything had to be step by step – fear, control, pain – though there might be a few extra specifics to throw into this day's work.

'I see you're with us at last,' he said, finally breaking the silence, and was rewarded with quick, ineffective movements from the man in front of him. A few mumbled sounds came from the bag over his face. Eddie reached out and patted him gently on the head, which responded by jerking violently from side to side. 'There, there son, no need to worry - not just yet anyhow,' he whispered menacingly. He paused, savouring the moment, and then slowly removed the patch from his eye socket. In one smooth motion he snatched the bag from the man's head.

Darren blinked quickly as he adjusted his eyes to the bright light suddenly assaulting them. A man's silhouette stood in front of him and slowly formed into a defined shape with recognisable features – too recognisable as he finally focused on the horribly deformed face of the R.U.C. Sergeant, Edward McQuillan, as it moved within inches of his own. Recoiling from the sight, and the reek of foul breath, Darren shrank his head backwards as far as he possibly could but he was restricted by something at his neck and couldn't escape the stench. He tried to fight his bonds, but he was held fast. Even the chair was bolted to the floor. He had no option but to stare into McQuillan's face and what he saw there was pure hatred. In that instant he knew he was a dead man.

'Hello McCann, I've been looking forward to our reunion,' McQuillan whispered, his voice barely more than a hiss. 'Do you know where you are?'

Darren swallowed but didn't try to speak, just shook his head slowly from side to side.

'Well, you're back in Ireland my fine lad, and you're in my care now,' McQuillan informed him. As he continued, his voice rose, word by word. 'You fucking ruined my life and my career in the R.U.C. A job guarding scum like you was the only work I could get - After You Fucking Blinded Me!' he ended on a scream, saliva drooling down his chin. He jumped back from the chair and spread his arms wide, circling as a maniacal laugh escaped his ruined face. 'Welcome to Her Majesty's Prison: Maze, McCann. You're in Long Kesh. You're in the fucking H-blocks.'

Darren reeled in disgust and fear as he stared at the mad man in front of him. His breath came in short, sharp bursts as he tried to assess his situation, to think of anything he could do or say to get himself out of this mess, but he knew he was done for. He could think of many people who had cause to hate him, but they were all dead and could do nothing about it. Now, in front of him, stood a very large, and very much alive, man with complete power over him. Worst of all, Darren knew it with absolute clarity as he looked into the one remaining eye; this man was completely insane. He had no idea what to expect, but McQuillan quickly left him in no doubt.

'The Bible tells us we must take an eye for an eye - and I am a devout man. I obey the word of God absolutely.' He licked the saliva from his chin before continuing in a voice that seemed to have no regular pattern, rising and falling, changing from laugh to hiss to shrill scream and back again. 'First I'm going to break both of your hands - every single fucking finger - every single fucking bone. Then I'm going to remove one of your eyes. I think I'll gouge it out - slowly - with my pen. Would you like to see the pen McCann?'

It was almost a girlish giggle that came from his mouth now as he slowly removed a fountain pen from his pocket and twirled it in front of his captive's face. Of all the sounds he'd heard over the last minute or so it was that giggle which terrified Darren the most and finally gave him back the ability to speak. 'Fuck you, you blind, mad bastard. You're a fucking head case. I should've finished you when I had the chance,' he screamed at the psychotic ex cop.

'Ah, I may very well be blind McCann, but you see - I'm only blind in one fucking eye - and I'm going to take both of yours.' He seemed to have regained control of his voice again as he added, 'but I think I'll only take one today. Don't want to get the fun over all in one go, do we?'

Darren was soaked with sweat and the tremors in his body were impossible to control, but he continued his efforts to loose himself from the bonds. Nothing. He couldn't move an inch. McQuillan slid behind him and he felt the rubbing on his wrist as one of his hands was freed. He tried to pull it in front of him but his arm was numb and he seemed to have no strength as McQuillan kept a firm, yet strangely gentle, grasp. He examined each of Darren's fingers in turn, massaging them until the circulation returned.

Darren stared in fascinated horror as McQuillan continued his ministrations. 'Which do you think would produce the most pain McCann, breaking your fingers first - or your fucking wrists?' he asked as he smirked at his panic-stricken captive.

Though it truly horrified him, Darren couldn't help but consider the question, and he shuddered at the images in his mind.

'I don't know what you think McCann, but I've a bit of experience here and I'm pretty sure the most painful thing would be to start with your fingers - then work my way up, don't you agree?' McQuillan continued in an almost friendly manner, still holding onto the hand.

Darren watched as his tormentor opened a drawer in the desk to his immediate left. He removed a small leather work bag and, making sure that Darren could see, began pulling out a succession of hand tools; chisels, screwdrivers and a selection of pliers, all the while gaily whistling "Protestant Men". He examined each tool with exaggerated consideration and finally settled on a claw hammer, then smiled at his captor in satisfaction. Darren attempted to return the gaze with defiance, but knew that he was trembling and betraying his fear. He'd felt fear before when facing an enemy, but that had been in a fair fight and had given him an adrenalin rush. Here he had no chance of retaliation and his thoughts went back to the Spanish thief and the similar position in which he had held him.

As McQuillan pushed his face once more into Darren's, he spat, 'Remember laddie, first your fingers, then your wrists

- then I might need a rest. Still, that should allow you to prepare for the next part, because then it'll be time for me to take one of your eyes.'

He paused a while, just watching McCann staring at him. This mental torture was almost as rewarding as the physical pain he was about to administer and it even made the loss of his eye seem worth it. Well, nearly. 'You don't have much to say for yourself, do you laddie?' he goaded.

'I'm not fucking telling you anything you crazy mad bastard,' screamed Darren, finally finding his voice.

'Hey, that's all right McCann. No worries. There's nothing you could tell me anyway, because there's nothing I want to know. The only thing I want is to break you, one little bit at a time - until you're fucking well dead,' laughed the ex R.U.C. man as he placed the clenched, captive hand on the desk in front of him and firmly prised it open, spreading the fingers.

It was true; Darren knew it. This wasn't an interrogation. This was revenge, pure and simple and, strangely, that realisation calmed him. He'd been on borrowed time long enough. The whole exile to Spain and then the hesitation with Ernesto, all of it letting him know his days were numbered. He should have listened to the inner warnings before now and got out while he could, and now it was too late. His end was to come at the hands of a madman and there was absolutely nothing he could do about it. Finally the defiance he'd been seeking filled his face and he stared up at the man. He made one last effort to remove his hand from McQuillan's grasp, but it was useless. Resigned to his fate, he sat and waited for the inevitable.

McQuillan noticed the change in the man's demeanour, and it was disappointing. This fear stage was supposed to go on longer – that was the routine. Why was this man suddenly ruining his perfect plan? The next stage was supposed to be savoured as he raised the hammer, slowly, holding it above the hand for long seconds. Instead, anger overtook him and he smashed the hammer down quickly, aiming for the thumb, but the blow glancing off the little finger.

Darren felt some small bones snap, but he gritted his teeth against the pain and continued to stare without uttering a sound. He saw the tendons rise on McQuillan's neck, his one eye appearing to turn red with rage. 'No!' Eddie finally screamed. 'It should be the thumb first. It's always the thumb first. Now I have to go backwards. Don't you see? You've made me go backwards.'

Darren had no idea what the man was babbling about, but he knew it wasn't good. He braced himself for another blow of the hammer, pretty sure that the next aim would be more effective, but McQuillan was still shouting out incoherent nonsense. 'It hasn't even gone right. See? It's not gone.'

What it was that hadn't gone became clear to Darren just a second later as McQuillan grabbed the little finger and twisted it viciously to complete the job half-started by his hammer. This time Darren could not stay quiet, the sound of grinding bones drowned out by his deep groan of pain. Broken bones were nothing new, but this was a sickening pain and the room spun as unconsciousness threatened for a second. 'Oh, God help me, I'll never get through this,' he thought. Then, as his focus returned, the hammer came down again, smashing across his knuckles as the whole hand collapsed and Darren passed out.

15

The Intrusion

When Darren came round again he wasn't sure where he was until the pain from his hand brought a fierce reminder. McQuillan was leaning against the wall, grinning and, as his victim came to, he approached again, hammer held high.

'Stop this at once, you bloody animal!' The loud, commanding voice came through the small grill in the cell door and McQuillan froze, his hammer in mid-air, as he heard the key grating in the lock. The door flew open and a scarlet-faced man entered followed by two unknown guards, battens held across their chests. Kenny Allen was behind them, key in hand, the look on his face showing quite clearly that he had no idea what he was supposed to do next. The young officer's glance flew to McQuillan, then at the red faced man and finally at the key, as if it bore all the responsibility for the position in which he had been placed. He attempted to make himself invisible.

'Put that hammer down!' was the next, barked order from the red-faced man.

'Who the fuck are you?' demanded McQuillan at the top of his voice, the hammer waving wildly in his hand. 'I gave strict orders no-one was to disturb me during this interrogation.' He glared at his fellow guard then, and Kenny shrank back against the wall.

'My name is Turner - and here is my I.D. Look at it man. Go on, look I said. And this so-called interrogation of yours is finished. It is terminated - do you bloody well hear me?'

McQuillan snatched the I.D. and examined it in anger before throwing it to the floor. He raised the hammer once more, but a well-aimed batten knocked it from his grasp.

'Go on, get out of here I said, and get out now man,' Turner ordered, his voice now more authoritarian than angry, a natural colour slowly returning to his face.

McQuillan looked around him wildly. This was his domain, his prisoner, his fucking revenge and he wasn't going anywhere.

'Eddie,' came the quiet voice from the shadows. 'There'll be another day, mate.'

Then Kenny Allen's hand was on his arm and he felt himself being led from the room as he gave one last, crazed look in the direction of Darren McCann. 'Cunt,' he whispered under his breath. 'I'll have you yet.'

Turner swallowed hard as he watched them leave. 'That intolerable little man,' he tutted. He loathed physical violence. He absolutely abhorred it and considered for the umpteenth time that he really was in the wrong job. Trouble was, he was good at it.

He made his way to the prisoner in the chair. This man had said nothing since his arrival and he just looked at him blankly now, offering no resistance as he examined the damaged hand. 'Get the doctor,' he ordered one of the guards behind him, before turning his attention back to the prisoner. 'I must say old man; this behaviour should never be tolerated in any of Her Majesty's Prisons. It's simply not on. I really do apologise.'

Darren stared back and said nothing. He was struggling to form his thoughts through the intense pain of his hand.

'Look old chap, I'll have a medic take care of that, give you some pain-killers, then we can have a little chat. Now how would that be?' He fished around in his pocket for a moment and produced his trusty old Swiss Army penknife. He bent low, hacking away with the short blade as he cut the sticky gaffer tape holding the prisoner down.

Darren stretched out his uninjured limbs, circling them to encourage the blood flow, but he remained silent. Turner seemed content with that for the moment and leaned against the wall, watching. The guard came back with the doctor who strapped the hand, administered pills and departed with such speed and efficiency, it was clearly a well-practiced routine. At a glance from their boss, the guards went out into the corridor and closed the door leaving the two men alone in the tiny cell.

Darren bit down on his good hand, trying to take some pain away from the other. He hoped those pills would kick in quickly. The strapping had helped but the throbbing continued and he didn't want to be distracted. His position had changed, though he doubted it was for the better. One thing was clear, this man was...'English,' he said, finally breaking the silence.

'What gave me away, old boy?' Turner smiled at him. When Darren didn't reply, he continued. 'Yes, English. Apologies for the awfully bad form. I really should introduce myself. The name is Turner, Anthony Turner and I work for the British Government as a - well that's not important now. And you are Darren, I believe, or do you prefer Butch? How about Mr. Butcher? Which is it to be?'

Darren slowly lifted his head and stared at the man. 'What's it to you?'

'Well, if we're to have a chat, we ought to be on civil terms, don't you think?'

'I've nothing to say to you, Englishman.'

'But I'm only here to help, you know. Seems I've helped already, wouldn't you say?' offered Turner, the smile still on his lips.

Darren's voice remained low as he spat, 'If you really want to help me, get the fuck out of my country. Leave Ireland for the Irish - you fucking British bastard.'

'Tut, tut, tut, there really is no need for that sort of language old chap,' replied Turner. 'I genuinely am here to help you know.'

'So, what the fuck do you want from me? You want me to grass - and inform on the boys do you?' mocked Darren.

'Actually - yes old boy, I do - that's exactly what I want to start with,' sighed Turner, ignoring the mocking tone.

The matter-of-fact reply caught him off guard and Darren heard himself laugh before controlling his voice once more. 'Well piss on you. Go and fuck yourself. Leave me alone you fucking British bastard.'

Turner closed his eyes and shook his head slowly before looking back at him benignly. 'Okay, for now I'm going to ignore the bad language. I used a little myself when I arrived, for which I apologise, and I know you've had a bad few days, Mr. Butcher.'

'Darren.'

'Sorry?'

'I prefer Darren.'

'Ah, yes, Darren it is then,' Turner agreed. 'Much better, I must admit. Butcher has all sorts of nasty connotations, doesn't it? Look here old chap, to ask the British to leave Northern Ireland is simply unrealistic. It'll never happen you see.'

'One day,' Darren assured him.

'Ah well, we'll agree to disagree on that one, then. Anyway, it seems to me you're more concerned with the Spanish these days. That was your kill, wasn't it, that poor devil they found yesterday in the bushes with his throat cut?'

Darren looked at him, but said nothing. He wasn't sure where this guy was getting his information, but it was unsettling.

'Don't worry, old boy. It looks as if the Spanish police are treating it as a robbery, and it's certainly none of our business. It just seemed a little strange to me. I thought you'd joined the I.R.A to avenge your mother's death and I don't really see what the poor old Spanish have done to you.'

At this Darren couldn't avoid the small gasp that escaped his lips but Turner didn't seem to pay it any attention, simply continuing in a gentle voice. 'I do wish you would consider answering me old bean. I guarantee that if you act in a more civil manner it really will be of great benefit to you - in the long run. Tell you what, how about we have a nice cup of tea?'

What the f...? This was surreal. Here he was, sitting in a torture chamber and this English cunt thought it was a good time for a cup of tea? He watched in disbelief as the man walked to the door and asked the guards to bring the drinks. He couldn't hear the reply but then Turner looked back in his direction. 'Won't be a mo,' he said. 'Looks like there's no room service.' And then he left.

Darren stared after him. This guy couldn't be for real, yet he'd seen for himself how quickly he'd dispatched McQuillan and he assumed he must have considerable authority to even get in here in the first place. His intelligence was obviously good and he wondered just how long the British government had been watching him. Shit, this wasn't good. It wasn't good at all. Right now Darren figured he'd rather be facing McQuillan again. At least you knew where you were with a murdering psychopath.

When the man reappeared a few moments later with two steaming mugs of tea, Darren raised his head slowly. 'Who the fuck are you?' he asked.

'I've already told you, old boy. I work for her Majesty. Now, I assumed you take milk and sugar,' said Turner, pulling over another chair to sit next to him.

Darren nodded and accepted the brew. He didn't want to take anything from this man and he certainly wasn't about to give up any information, but that tea was simply too tempting to his parched throat.

They drank in silence for a while, until Turner finally pressed, 'So, am I right? Did you join the I.R.A. to avenge your mother's death?'

There was clearly no point in lying and he certainly wasn't ashamed of his motives. 'Aye, I fucking did,' he answered through clenched teeth. 'I joined to kill the Prods and Brits. They murdered my mammy, and I'm going to kill as many of them as I fucking can.'

Inwardly cringing at the profanities this man bandied about with ease, Turner tried his best to ignore them. Casually pulling out a pack of cigarettes from his pocket he offered McCann one. Darren took the cigarette and broke off the filter before accepting the light. Turner narrowed his eyes in concentration. He should have remembered that. He'd seen that trait a few times in similar young men of this persuasion. For some reason they preferred their cigarettes unfiltered. Mental note logged, he continued with the business at hand. 'So, Mr. McCann, I am authorised by Her Majesty's Government to offer you an amnesty.'

'Fuck you,' snapped Darren, turning his face away.

'Please allow me to finish before interrupting again, if you would be so kind, Mr. McCann,' Turner continued, friendly, benign, unflappable smile still in place. 'This amnesty would, naturally, cover all of your previous crimes, but it will only be given in return for your total and complete co-operation.' He held up his hand to forestall the dismissive reply he saw forming on Darren's lips. 'Not until I've finished, remember?

'In short, sir, we wish to be made aware of everything that you know about the Provisional I.R.A. Its safe houses, smuggling routes, weapons storage locations, etcetera, etcetera. In fact, we need the whole picture in as far as you see and understand things. In return for this information you will, of course, be provided with a new identity, a safe house in rural England and a motor vehicle - a rather nice Jaguar actually. Plus, of course, you will receive a salary. This salary will be set equal to a level EO civil servant and your expenses will be covered.

'Obviously you will be required to pay income tax on this salary. However, any special work you perform for Her Majesty will be recompensed tax-free. And that special work is something we will need to discuss. There, I have now paused. You may ask your questions.'

Darren dragged slowly on the last of his cigarette, eyeing the man closely. 'So,' he said, a rueful smile on his lips, 'you want information and you're offering me a job? Is that right?

'Spot on, old chap.'

Darren casually threw the cigarette end to the floor and slowly crushed it beneath his feet. 'Well,' he said, 'in response to such a kind offer, I can only repeat: Go fuck yourself.'

'Mr. McCann, this profanity really is unnecessary.'

'GO - FUCK - YOURSELF,' Darren repeated, enunciating each word for effect.

'Have it your way, Mr. McCann, but before you dismiss the idea of working for Her Majesty's Government, you do need to be made aware of certain facts - one of which may well change your thought process, along with your loyalties.'

'And, as I've already told you, fuck off, I've nothing more to say.'

The smile had slowly faded from Turner's lips to be replaced by a serious, almost sad, expression. 'Mr. McCann, Darren, there is something you need to know, and it won't be easy for you to hear.'

'You can't tell me anything I don't already know, you idiotic English cunt,' Darren spat at him. He paused and sighed. 'Look, I'm not stupid. I know what you want and I know the position I'm in. It's over for me, but I'll die before I tell you anything. I was ready to die before you got here and I'm still ready. If you really want to help me, like you say, then put a bullet in my head now. I'd really rather not face that madman McQuillan again. I don't know how you train 'em, but he is, one-hundred-percent, in-fucking-sane.'

'We do agree on one thing, then,' Turner confirmed. 'I really do sincerely apologise for that, old chap. You weren't supposed to be here, you know. Some clerical error. You were supposed to be in our headquarters.'

'Would that have been a better class of torture chamber, then?'

'Well, we do have tea making facilities in the room,' Turner offered.

Darren allowed himself one genuine smile at that. 'Aye, everything's better with a nice cup of tea,' he agreed. 'Look Turner, why are we wasting each other's time? You've done your research, you know plenty about me and I'm not going to deny anything you've said. No point. But if you know so much, then you know I'm not going to break. Kill me now and then you can go back to drinking your fu... er, flipping tea.'

'No, Darren, I can't do that. Not until you have all the facts,'

'Go on then, since we're all nice and chatty like you wanted. What is it? What's this startling piece of information you have for me?'

Turner shuffled in his chair, edging it closer to Darren and laying a hand on his knee. It was an odd gesture, but Darren ignored it. 'I'm sorry, son,' Turner began, ' but you've been lied to and you've been used.'

Darren stiffened and moved to throw the man's hand from his leg, but Turner strengthened his grip, squeezing the knee. 'You need to hear this,' he said softly. 'Your mother was not killed by the British, or the U.V.F or any...'

'Fuck you,' Darren began.

'LISTEN TO ME!' Turner raised his voice for the first time and surprised Darren to silence. 'She was not killed by any Protestant group or any British affiliation in any form,' Turner continued, his voice immediately low and controlled once more. 'She was murdered by your very own organisation, son, the Provisional I.R.A.'

Darren stared at the man opposite him, his eyes narrowing, the taste of bile rising to his throat as he grappled with such a dirty trick. Did this idiot before him really think this would work? Did he honestly believe that using his sainted mother for a pawn in his evil game would win him over? The stupid, cruel...

His anger boiled over then. 'Fuck you, you lying British bastard,' he yelled, lurching to his feet and turning over the desk next to them, crashing his injured hand into the side. 'AARGH, JESUS FUCKING CHRIST, FUCK ME, THAT FUCKING HURTS,' he screamed at the top of his lungs as the searing pain coursed through his body.

Turner physically recoiled in his chair and the door flew open as the guards rushed in.

'Shit, Bastard, Fuck,' Darren continued, holding his arm to his chest and dancing round in agony.

Turner quickly recovered, dismissing the guards with a frantic wave of his hand and rushing to Darren's side. 'Deep breaths, deep breaths, old man,' he advised as he held him by the shoulders. 'That has got to sting.'

'Sting? Sting? Fuck me,' said Darren, squeezing his eyes together as he waited for the pain to subside.

'Yes, well, under the circumstances, I can understand the swearing...'

'And fuck you,' Darren returned. 'You and your British lies. How dare you use my mother like that? How fucking dare you?' God, his hand hurt, but maybe it was just what he needed to focus his mind. He'd let this man get under his skin a bit. Time to put an end to that.

Turner took a few steps back. 'I see you are not convinced.' Darren's cold stare suggested he didn't even think that worthy of a reply, and Turner nodded slowly. 'Yes, personally, I don't blame you. Not without proof anyway. I would insist on hard, irrefutable proof too, were I in your position. Would you like that proof, Mr. McCann?'

'You have no fucking proof because it's all lies,' Darren spat at him. 'I know how my mammy was killed. I know the signatures. I know who did it.'

'Yes, well I can see how you would think that, but...'

'Get the fuck out of my sight,' Darren hissed.

'I'm afraid you're in no position to issue the orders here, Mr. McCann. Have you forgotten where you are? You will listen to this proof. You have no choice.' Turner's voice was once more low and commanding.

'I'm not listening to another word from your lying mouth,' Darren threw at him.

'No, no, not me, old bean, I'm done for a while. There's someone else you should listen to.'

Darren blinked and took a step backwards. 'Who? You got someone else here to try to fuck with my brain?'

'Please bear with me,' Turner continued. 'Now, I told you this would be difficult to hear, but hear it you must.'

Until then, Darren hadn't noticed the briefcase standing against the wall. Turner reached into it now and produced a cassette player. He righted the desk and set the device upon it. 'You should sit,' he advised, and Darren followed the instruction as he experienced his first moment of doubt. Turner sat next to him, smiled sadly, and pressed "Play".

A hard, Belfast accent emitted from the machine, and Turner watched Darren's reaction. 'I see you recognise this man's voice,' he said quietly. Darren slowly nodded his head. He knew the voice all right. It was Johnny O'Leary, a trusted, well known and hard-core member of the Provisional I.R.A. More than that, he'd been a close childhood friend. A year above him at school, he'd always seemed "likely to succeed" in his chosen profession. Darren sat in silence as he listened to his friend reel off a list of his crimes. It was a very long list.

Obviously he had been turned and was in the process of gaining an amnesty of his own. Hard as that was to believe, Darren maintained a neutral expression as the voice continued. Then, his jaw dropped and his eyes flew wide open at the mention of one particular killing.

'Douglas James Mallone - shot in the head. Order issued by Falls Road Brigade. Kill order approved by the committee, Belfast,' said the voice.

Darren winced, and the reactive 'Fuck me,' escaped his lips before he had time to stop it.

Turner paused the recording. 'You knew that man?' he asked.

'I've known a lot of people who are now dead,' Darren recovered quickly, and it was true. But this was Duggy he was hearing about: Thomas' younger brother, a republican through and through. Of course he already knew Duggy was gone, Thomas had told him, but why would his own side have killed him? He managed to keep the thought to himself.

'Shall I continue?' Turner asked.

Darren nodded. He didn't want to hear any of this, but now he knew he needed to listen to the rest of that tape, not that Turner was giving him any choice in the matter.

The recording started again and the voice continued. The next couple of names meant nothing to him, but then Darren froze as the voice reported, 'Mary Jeanette McCann, throat cut. Order issued by Crossmaglen. Kill order approved by the committee, Belfast.'

Turner stopped the playback and looked at the man in front of him, the face frozen. 'I genuinely am sorry old chap,' he whispered as he stood. 'I'll organise some more tea for us, eh? No doubt you'll be needing a few moments alone to consider things.' Slowly he left the room and the door was locked behind him.

Darren felt the colour drain from his face and a tremor ran through his body as he sat in stunned silence. At first his mind went blank and he found it impossible to construct a thought. Then, slowly, the words from the tape seeped back into his consciousness. The guards in the corridor remained with their backs to the door as they heard the long, low animalistic wail. It was the sound of a tortured and deeply damaged soul.

When Turner eventually returned he was carrying tea and had managed to rustle up some biscuits from somewhere. He kicked the door shut behind him and laid the fare in front of Darren. 'Not sure when you last ate, son.' Neither was Darren, and he was suddenly starving. He wolfed down several biscuits in silence.

'Fucking murdering bastards,' he screamed at one point to no one in particular, and then he was quiet again. Turner sat patiently and waited. He'd played most of his cards and was confident of his position, but the next move belonged to his opponent. And this was one scary man, Turner had to admit.

The silence continued and it was going on too long. Turner's instinct, combined with long experience, warned him that they were at a dangerous pass. The tension and anger in the man opposite him were obvious and understandable, but there was something more and Turner decided he had to force the issue.

'Would you care for another cigarette Mr. McCann?' he offered, thrusting a pack of Senior Service, plain, no filter, towards him as he silently thanked that Kenny Allen lad for his choice of brand.

Darren considered the pack for several seconds. Then, with trembling fingers, he took a cigarette, lit it and sat with his eyes tightly closed, a single tear rolling down his cheek. His lips began to move, though no sound escaped them, but Turner knew the moment was approaching and he afforded himself a moment of congratulation as he waited for his latest defection. Stupid, he realised just one second later.

'Lies.' The word was so quietly spoken that Turner wasn't sure he had caught it.

'What was that, Mr. McCann?'

'Lies!' Darren repeated, more audibly this time as he raised his head and stared at the man opposite.

Turner felt himself recoil at what he saw in those eyes. The anger was to be expected, but this anger was directed at him, he could feel it. He had only a second to react before Darren lunged in his direction and he narrowly avoided a punch to the face. 'Guards,' he yelled, and the door flew open, the two large men rushing to grab Darren before he could strike again.

'Lying English cunts,' Darren yelled as he struggled in the arms of the men holding him. 'You made that tape yourself. You must think I'm a fucking idiot. Jonny O'Leary? Holy fucking Christ, he'd never turn. Never!'

Turner was at the door. 'Leave him,' he ordered the guards. Within seconds Darren was alone in the cell once more.

Over the next few hours the Englishman returned to the cell several times, but he didn't enter, simply observing Darren through the grill. He had badly mistimed his last visit and he wasn't about to make that mistake again. There was an ace he still had to play but he had so hoped to avoid it. It seemed too cruel beyond measure, and Turner wasn't a cruel man. Beyond that, it was dangerous. He watched as Darren paced the tiny cell, ranting like a mad man at the walls. 'Fucking Shankill Butchers, that's who,' he deciphered from one visit and "Every fucking Brit,' from another. The recording hadn't done the job he had hoped and Turner considered his last remaining move. If that didn't work, then Mr. Darren McCann would not receive the bullet to his head that he had requested. Instead he would stay exactly where he was, no clerical error involved this time. He would become an inmate of Her

Majesty's Prison: Maze, once again at the mercy of that madman McQuillan.

One of the guards summoned him for another visit to the cell and Turner observed Darren seated once more, slowly rocking back and forth in the chair. All was finally quiet. It was disturbing to Anthony Turner to see a man so horribly broken, but that was his job and this time he was sure he was judging his moment correctly.

Darren was exhausted and raised his head wearily as the door opened. Turner entered first, but it was the second man who caused him to jump from his seat in panic. 'No, man, no,' he managed in ragged breaths as he staggered back towards the wall.

'Sit down, Butch, I've something to tell you,' Jonny O'Leary said quietly.

Turner walked silently from the room.

'What the fuck, Jonny?' Darren began as he sank slowly back into the chair. 'Those bastards told me it was you who killed my mammy - but I don't believe a fucking word. They fabricated that fucking tape, I know it.'

'You will hear me out before you say anything, won't you Butch?' and in those quietly spoken words from a friend, Darren knew the truth. His head fell to his hands, all fight gone from him as his body began to shake with his sobs.

'I had no choice, Butch,' Jonny continued, his voice barely above a whisper. 'It was a direct order from Cross and Belfast. You know what happens if you disobey a direct order, Butch. You're gone, disappeared. I could have taken that, man, for me, but it was my family, mate. They threatened my family.'

Darren raised his head to look at his friend, but said nothing as Jonny went on, his voice rising now, the plea obvious in his tone. 'I'm so fucking sorry, Butch. You know how much I liked your mam. It's haunting me mate. I can't fucking sleep. I didn't give a shit about the others. Not even poor Duggy. He'd turned, you know, they were sure of it. But your mammy? All these years it's got worse. It won't leave me. It won't go away.'

'It won't leave you?' Darren finally managed through his sobs. 'You can't sleep? You, you, you! What about me? What about fucking me?'

' I know man, I know.'

'You know fucking nothing,' Darren hissed. He took short sharp breaths, controlling his sobs, feeling the anger grow inside him once more. 'Why? Just tell me that. Fucking why?'

'I don't know, Butch. Honest, mate, I don't.'

'Don't call me mate and don't call me Butch,' growled Darren, slowly rising to his feet.

Jonny backed away. 'Okay, okay,' he sputtered. 'Look Bu... Darren. I've asked myself, man. I've asked myself why, but I don't fucking know. It makes no sense to me, man, and that's why I'm here.'

Darren stared at him and Jonny, now with his back to the wall, raised his palms defensively. 'I came to them man. These Brits, they didn't come for me. I came to them. And it was 'cause of your mammy Bu...'

He wasn't allowed to finish as Darren lunged at him, grabbing him by the throat and squeezing with all his might. O'Leary made no attempt to defend himself as he sank to the floor, but the door flew open and the guards were immediately on top of them, pulling Darren off and forcing him back to the chair, holding him firmly. Jonny O'Leary slowly crawled to the door, gasping for air, then rose to his feet.

'Why the beating? Why the knife?' Darren screamed from his confinement. 'Why the fucking knife?'

Jonny looked back at him, but could only shake his head.

'I'll fucking kill you,' the screaming continued. 'I'm gonna fucking skin you alive. You'll be begging me to end your life when I've done, you fucking bastard.'

The door closed and Jonny was gone.

The guards continued to hold him down until he stopped thrashing in his seat and the sobs overtook him once more. At a nod through the grill from Turner, they left him and Darren was alone again. At some point a meal was pushed through the door, but no one came to see him. He rocked back and forth in his chair, then moved to the floor, curling into a ball like a small child, sobbing out his grief for his mother and for the betrayal he now knew was real. When there were no sobs left, exhaustion finally brought sleep.

The door opened the following - morning? Afternoon? Night? He had no idea. There was no light in the cell and time had lost all meaning to him, along with most of his life. At Turner's entrance, Darren fixed him with dark, sad eyes and offered just one word. 'Why?'

'I can't say for sure, my boy,' Turner confessed, his heart touched by the sheer dejection he heard in the young man's voice. 'My best guess is that they wanted you and that was the only way they knew how. Had they tried to recruit you before?'

'Aye.'

'And you wouldn't give in?'

'No.'

'Well, you are a hard nut to crack, Mr. McCann.'

At Darren's accusatory glare, Turner quickly continued. 'I really am so genuinely sorry it had to come to that.'

Darren nodded his head. Though he no longer knew what to believe, he felt that much was true. 'How long have you known?' he asked. 'About my mammy that is.'

'Not long. Not for sure, anyway. We didn't have any proof until O'Leary came to us.'

'I'm going to kill him; him and the rest of those treacherous bastards.'

'I don't doubt it for a moment,' Turner assured him, though he inwardly believed it would prove difficult to find Jonny O'Leary. At this very moment, he was being whisked away to parts unknown.

'I'm hungry,' said Darren.

The normal, every day statement took Turner by surprise, but it was the breakthrough moment and he knew it. He looked to the corner of the room and saw the cold, congealed, uneaten food that had been delivered some time earlier. 'Oh my dear boy, you must be famished. I'll get something sorted for you immediately.' After a quick word with the guards he was back at Darren's side, knowing he must press his advantage right now. 'Shall we have a look at some paperwork while we wait?' he suggested. 'It's all a bit of a pain, I's dotted, T's crossed, that sort of thing,' he mumbled as he removed documents from his case, not wanting to pause and give Darren too much time to think about it.

'As I said previously, we would really value your services old boy. You have intricate, specialist knowledge you see. You know detailed information of the operations here in Ireland, and also the routes to and from mainland Europe. You have direct contacts in Spain, France, Belgium, and possibly, other countries too. Work for us, and you'll get everything I promised.' Turner placed the documents on the desk

Darren sighed. 'You really have done your homework,' he admitted, taking the offered pages and beginning to read.

He broke off when his meal arrived, ate hungrily, and then read some more. He saw in black and white the details of a house, payment and that shiny new Jaguar that had been mentioned. He saw, too, the carefully worded "specialist duties" he would be asked to perform. A hit man by any other name, he knew. Something approaching a small smile touched his lips as he finished the document. 'So, I'm trading one set of murdering bastard masters for another, then?'

'Mr. McCann, I really do have to object to all this profanity,' Turner began, but Darren cut him short.

'Do you know what the I.R.A. would do to me if they found out?' he asked, then caught himself with a humourless laugh. 'What do I mean, "if"? They probably already know, don't they?'

'There's a chance, dear boy,' Turner acknowledged, 'but I think we've got it covered.'

'So you're asking me to risk my fucking life for you and you object to the odd swear word?'

'It's more than the odd word, old bean. Really, it is terribly offensive, you know.'

'Well I am most *terribly* sorry, *old bean*, if I give offence,' Darren mimicked. 'Look, I'll make you a deal. I'll watch my mouth if you will tell me when I get to kill those fu… er, nasty fellows who I've worked for all these fu… - all these years.'

Turner smiled and nodded. 'It's a deal,' he agreed.

'So, if I sign these papers, when do I get to finish my mammy's killers?'

'Okay, okay, all in good time, my dear fellow. First we will need some information from you, as I've already outlined, then we will move to the more, er, specialist duties and you will have to follow some orders. We can't have our operatives running wild, killing who they like willy nilly, now can we? That would be quite unseemly.'

'Quite,' Darren agreed.

Turner ignored the sarcasm of the interruption and continued. 'You will only terminate carefully selected targets. I'm sure your old colleagues will eventually be selected, but first there are more pressing matters.'

'Like what?' Darren asked flatly.

'Well, and this is only one example,' Turner offered, 'we urgently need to stem the flow of money and arms to several Irish terrorist groups. And as the majority of these goods seem to originate in the United States of America, I would imagine your first terminations would be carried out over there - not here in Ireland my boy.'

Darren returned his gaze to the papers in front of him. It was all so official, all so fucking sanitised, though he kept the words to himself. He was really sitting here considering signing up to work for the British government, a body he had hated for so long. Yet, what choice did he have? His hatred now had a different target and really, honestly, this looked like the best, the only, way to get his revenge.

'So, old bean, what is it to be? A yea or a nay?' Turner pressed.

'People really talk like that?' Darren mused. Then he sighed and picked up the pen. 'Fuck it,' he said. 'Let's take a look at that Jaguar.'

'Mr. McCann. Really.'

'Sorry,' mumbled Darren as he signed his life away.

Turner took the papers from him. 'A wise decision, son,' he thought as he passed a brown paper package across the desk. 'Your possessions,' he said, 'then we need to talk about the next step.'

Darren looked inside the parcel and quickly pocketed a pack of cigarettes and his lighter and cradled *The Killer* in his palm. The rest of his personal items he dropped directly into the waste bin.

He followed Turner out of the cell and the watery light of early morning seeped through the corridor windows to offer him the first glimpse of sunlight he had seen since driving the little Honda through Spain. It saddened him to realise that he could never return that car to its owner, the wizened old lady who had come to mean so much to him. He didn't know how long it had been since his abduction and he wondered if she and her boys knew what had happened to him. Yes, they probably did, at least in part. They would eventually find the crashed car and he thought Vassi, for sure, would be able to put the pieces together. Oh, how he missed his brothers in arms and he longed to be back with them.

The weight of the Killer in his hand, and the feeling of the Spanish lettering along the side, only served to deepen that longing as he and Turner arrived at another door. When it opened he looked out into a large yard, with trees in the distance beyond a tall fence, and the need for freedom overwhelmed him.

16

The Shooting

As Eddie McQuillan arrived for work that morning he parked in his spot and emptied the contents of his ashtray into one of the neatly folded paper bags he carried for the purpose. He exited the car, locked the doors and walked round the vehicle checking that everything was secure and wiping down each handle in turn. 'There, nice and clean again,' he whispered. He walked to the main entrance, depositing his rubbish in the bin as he passed, then entered his domain.

For the last two days he had incorporated new rituals into his routine, and they were working out well. He didn't really like anything new, but since his last interrogation had been so rudely interrupted, he had to prepare himself. Everything had to be perfect so that he was ready to take over again. He now arrived an hour early for his shift and spent the first thirty minutes on an exacting routine in the gym. He counted his reps aloud in groups of three; happy in the order they brought to his mind. Then he would have a close shave and take a scalding hot shower. With precisely fifteen minutes left before his shift began he had the kettle boiling while he dressed in his freshly laundered and perfectly pressed uniform. Then he would make his tea and take it with him through to the office.

He was sitting at his desk finishing the last of his tea when Kenny Allen entered. 'Someone got a good dose this morning,' the young officer informed him. 'Just heard that another of those bastards is dead. Shot trying to escape about an hour ago.'

McQuillan smiled as he rose to check his appearance one last time in the mirror before the two men headed out across the yard to the wing. The stench of the yard made Allen gag every time, but McQuillan loved it. It was the stink of his domain, the smell of power and he relished it.

The warden was walking towards them as they approached the wing. This man was his only superior here, and Eddie was surprised to see him. He was usually locked away in his office, and that's when he was even on the premises. Today he looked unhappy. 'Paperwork,' he announced as he reached his juniors.

'The attempted escape, sir?' questioned Kenny.

'Yes, but this one's a fucking celebrity, and I didn't even know we had him in our nick. How's that going to look, eh?' He marched off muttering, "Fucking Butcher of Belfast.'

Kenny saw the colour drain from McQuillan's face and became quickly concerned as the man stumbled, looking ready to collapse. 'Eddie, you going to be okay, man?' he asked. Eddie honestly didn't think he was. He felt physically ill. 'Let's get you back to the office, eh?' said Kenny, already shepherding him in that direction and Eddie offered no resistance.

Within minutes Kenny had him seated and the kettle was on. He was really worried. The man looked truly ill. Of course he knew that it was the Butcher who had taken McQuillan's eye, everyone knew, so he understood the personal connection, but this reaction seemed extreme. 'Eddie, man,' he began.

'Bastard,' cried McQuillan, the piercing shriek stopping Kenny in his tracks. 'McCann was supposed to be mine. He was not intended for some fucking squaddie to use as fucking target practice. What the fuck am I going to do now?'

'He's gone, Eddie,' offered Kenny, knowing it was a stupid thing to say, but at a loss for anything else.

'I know he's fucking gone, you twat,' McQuillan spat in his face. 'McCann you fucking bastard, I hope you rot in fucking Hell - for fucking ever.'

Allen watched as tears fell from the lone eye. 'Jesus,' he muttered. 'Eddie, calm down mate. The man's dead - there's nothing you can do about it. I know you wanted him for yourself, but he's gone mate, he's dead, face it. He is dead.'

'You fucking know that bastard was mine, no one else's - he was mine,' McQuillan hissed.

'Aye, I know that mate, but at least he's dead. It's not like he escaped or anything - is it?'

Eddie stared at him and, just as quickly as they had come, the tears stopped and he grinned. 'You know, you're right, he is dead. Fuck him.' he replied calmly.

Allen risked a cautious smile as he looked at his friend. 'Unbelievable,' he thought, but never said a word. It only took a split second for him to change from that screaming, rabid lunatic, back into a calm rational human being. Inwardly Allen shuddered. 'Fuck me,' he thought. 'I knew Eddie had his problems. But Jesus, now he's really starting to scare me.'

'Well then,' McQuillan announced, 'back to work.'

Kenny watched him stride off back through the yard. 'Shit,' he said. 'He's finally lost it.'

Word of the latest shooting quickly made its way round the H-Blocks. The Protestants were cheering while the Provos mourned the loss of yet another brother. Several times during the day a fellow officer would pass by and pat McQuillan on the shoulder. 'We've got him for you mate,' was the general feeling of congratulatory brotherhood, and McQuillan would grin widely and agree that it was, indeed, a great day.

In the early afternoon a helicopter landed just outside the prison walls and was seen leaving again a short time later. 'Looks like we've got rid of that English bastard too,' McQuillan noted with glee. 'This day just keeps getting better and better.'

Kenny Allen watched closely and was concerned. If he hadn't witnessed the original reaction he probably wouldn't have thought anything of it, but this excessive mood-swing unsettled him. As they finally walked together from the prison at the end of their shift, Kenny suggested, 'Hey, fancy a pint Eddie?'

'No can do,' replied McQuillan. 'Not tonight I'm afraid.' He got in his car and left with a cheery wave.

'Pity, I reckon a couple of pints would have done him good,' thought Kenny as he headed for his own car and then to his favourite pub. It was only 6pm, with the sun just beginning to set, and a little early for his daily tipple, but Kenny felt in need of an extra beer that evening.

When Edward "Eddie" McQuillan didn't show up for work the next day a call to his landlady resulted in the news that he had been found at home, naked, service pistol in hand and a gaping hole through what had once been his good eye. On the table next to him, neatly ordered rags and light oil suggested the pistol had received a thorough cleaning first.

17

England, 1981

As the helicopter touched down a few hours after the infamous Butcher of Belfast had attempted to escape, Turner sighed with relief. He couldn't wait to leave this place. The incidents there had saddened him and, since the shooting, he'd had to listen to the cheers and wails that echoed menacingly off the prison walls. He really couldn't think straight with all those emotions going on around him. It wasn't until the helicopter took off and the only sound was the loud, yet somehow hypnotic, whir of the blades that he began to focus again. It had been a truly terrible couple of days and he was keen to get back to his little antique shop and once more become the sad, quiet

Englishman whom everyone ignored. He'd have to spend a bit of time in England first, but he would be home soon. He was English through and through, but that tiny corner of Dublin had become his sanctuary.

The two guards who had accompanied him had been separately dispatched and the only other occupant of the helicopter was Mr. O'Neil, who was considering the paperwork that Turner had given him. 'Shame,' his fellow passenger yelled above the din of the chopper. Turner nodded to agree that it was, indeed, a shame, accepted the returned paperwork, placed it in his briefcase and then settled back to try to sleep. Conversation really wasn't an option.

After just two days in blighty, Anthony Turner prepared for his last meeting before he could leave. He was to see Liam O'Neil again, and then he could go home. He had the tea ready brewing as the secretary brought in his guest. A brief handshake and they got straight down to business. 'So you've seen the file on Ryan McKee?' Turner asked.

'Yes. So he's not the head of N.O.R.A.I.D then?'

'No, but as controller of the Manhattan branch, he's certainly a fellow of great interest,' Turner assured him. 'Here are the rest of the documents you require.'

His visitor accepted the package and fumbled to open the passport with one hand, his other hampered by a sling. 'Fuck me,' he said.

'Mr. McCann, please,' protested Turner.

'Sorry,' said Darren, as he placed the passport on the desk and idly fingered the scar on his check. 'And don't you think we'd better keep it to Liam O'Neil from now on. Darren McCann is dead, remember.'

'Indeed he is, Mr. O'Neil. Indeed he is,' Turner agreed.

The End...
But only of The Beginning

The Ambient E
By Michael Swanson

When a mysterious caller's song requests are aired on a radio show fronted by a hate spitting DJ *who doesn't play requests* ... people start dying, or coming back to life, and some just go plain crazy.

Across the world, an American musician on tour in the UK finds a cache of ancient sheet music that, when played, may have the power to change the destiny of the world. It's all in the music - the truth, the devil, the secret of everything.

Is the song of the universe tuned to The Ambient E? Is Led Zeppelin's *Stairway to Heaven* a slippery slide to Hell? Why is the Pope suspicious of Bob Dylan? Michael Swanson's breathtaking rock-n-roll novel may have the answer. And it is will certainly change your life.

Find out more at: www.yellowbay.co.uk

The Second Rule

By Clifford Thurlow

When Tomas Sala, state architect to the dictator, finds himself alone one night with an aching nostalgia and a steady supply of booze, he begins to re-evaluate his life, a catharsis that makes him realize there is something vital that he must do. He thinks of his cellist wife Helena, now in exile, of his son, now dead, and of his own childhood marred by tragedy. He remembers his time as a student, designing the aberration that will become the Palace of Democracy, whilst listening to the sounds of his friend Anton expertly seducing yet another virgin next door. While Tomas Sala is able to build the absurd vision of his leader, his personal dreams disintegrate. His journey into the past begins to set out a path to action and, ultimately, perhaps, to his own salvation...

Find out more at: www.yellowbay.co.uk

Made in the USA
San Bernardino, CA
17 March 2014